21 GAY STREET

LAWRENCE BLOCK
WRITING AS SHELDON LORD

21 GAY STREET

Lawrence Block writing as Sheldon Lord

Copyright © 1960 Lawrence Block

All Rights Reserved.

Cover and Interior Design by QA Productions

A LAWRENCE BLOCK PRODUCTION

Classic Erotica

21 Gay Street
Candy
Gigolo Johnny Wells
April North
Carla
A Strange Kind of Love
Campus Tramp
Community of Women
Born to be Bad
College for Sinners
Of Shame and Joy
A Woman Must Love
The Adulterers
The Twisted Ones
High School Sex Club
I Sell Love
69 Barrow Street
Four Lives at the Crossroads
Circle of Sinners
A Girl Called Honey
Sin Hellcat
So Willing

Classic Erotica #1

21 GAY STREET

LAWRENCE BLOCK

CHAPTER 1

The cabdriver, a short stubby man named Irving Goldin, picked up the fare at the Grayhound terminal at 50th Street and Eighth Avenue. He helped her with her suitcase, then hopped into his seat and headed the cab downtown along Seventh Avenue. It was almost four-thirty in the afternoon, the start of the rush hour, and traffic was heavy. Cars moved slowly along the wide street. It was June and hot, and Irving Goldin, who was carrying a little too much weight on his stocky frame, was sweating freely. It was not only a hot day but a humid one as well, and the sweat remained where it was instead of evaporating. Irving Goldin was uncomfortable.

At 42nd Street one idiot made a left turn from the right-hand lane while another idiot helped things along by attempting a right turn from the left-hand lane. Irving Goldin cursed, gently because his fare was female, and bided his time. The light turned, and this time he managed to head the cab across the intersection.

34th Street was, if possible, worse. The cars were piled up and it took two changes of the light before the cab got across the street. Goldin cursed a bit, experimentally, and then began to study his passenger in the rear view mirror. The mirror was slightly clouded, a violation which no cop had spotted thus far, but even so Irving Goldin got a good look at his fare.

She was a very beautiful girl.

Her hair was jet black, shoulder length, hanging loose. She had a high forehead and a clear, light complexion. Her eyes were almond shaped, dark brown and quite large. She had a full mouth with only the slightest trace of lipstick on her lips.

The light turned green and a horn behind him reminded Goldin that he was supposed to be driving, not watching women. He pressed down violently on the gas pedal and shot across the street. Only half his mind was on his driving. The other half was on the girl in the back seat.

A pretty one, he thought. Twenty, twenty-one, twenty-two—somewhere around there. Tough to tell their ages nowadays, but there was no question about this one, she was young. And something worth looking at. He tried to remember what her body had looked like. It was an easy body to remember. It went with the face—long legs, slender hips, a flat stomach, good large breasts.

"A hot day," Goldin remarked.

There was no answer from the girl.

"Hot," he went on. "Though you know what it is they say: it's not the heat so much as the humidity. One way or the other, it's a hot one, all right."

The girl didn't say anything.

Goldin shrugged. Evidently the only way to get an answer out of her was to ask her a question. Well, what the hell.

"21 Gay Street," he said aloud. "That's the address where you're going, isn't it?"

"That's right."

"That's in the Village," he said. "Greenwich Village. Right?"

"That's right."

She had a nice enough voice, he decided. Mellow, sort of. Even if she didn't have a hell of a lot to say.

"The Village," he went on. "Winding twisting streets. Never can find my way around there. Always keep getting lost. Bad as Brooklyn that way, almost."

Silence from the back seat. He looked in the mirror, found a face devoid of expression.

"But," he went on, "it's supposed to be an interesting place. What I hear, anyway. Never spent much time there myself. Bronx is good enough for me. Some people, though, I guess they like it down there. In the Village, I mean."

"I suppose so."

"Hear it's pretty wild," he said. "You know, you hear a lot. Most of it's probably a lot of nonsense, but you hear a lot. Beatniks, free love, queers, you know. Things like that."

More silence.

"In the papers," Goldin sailed on, unable to restrain himself. "You know, like the cops make a raid and arrest a lot of people for selling dope or something. Or a bunch of bearded guys picket a church or something. Maybe it's publicity, I don't know, but you hear a lot."

More silence. The cab went steadily south, across 23rd Street, across 14th Street. The traffic got progressively lighter. The street was still thronged with cars, but traffic moved along at a steadier pace now.

"14th Street," Goldin announced. "We're in the Village. Officially, that is."

The girl didn't say anything.

"The way I figure it," Goldin said, "a man has a right to do what he wants. Long as he don't bother anybody, that is. For instance, I got a brother. A half-brother, actually. My father died and my old lady remarried and they had this kid, he's what you call my half-brother. About six years younger than me. Anyway, he's an alcoholic. Not a bum, you understand. What it is, he drinks. Like a fish, more or less. He'll knock off a quart a day of bonded rye."

A sports car, a red MG with top down and wheels screaming, cut in on the cab. Goldin hit the brake hard, missed the MG, swore automatically, then took a breath.

"Anyway," he went on, "this brother, half-brother, that is— people keep saying how terrible it is. How he drinks, I mean. But who's he hurting? He don't beat his wife, he makes good money, holds onto his job, does his drinking at home so he don't fall over on the street. Way I look at it, maybe he's got a reason to drink. It's his business. And it's the same with these beatniks."

The clarity of that little message was, for the moment, lost even on Goldin. He thought for a minute or two, retraced his words, and figured out what he was talking about.

"What I mean," he said, "they want beards, let 'em have beards. They want free love, let 'em have free love. They're hurting somebody? Leave 'em be, for the love of God. Right?"

No answer.

"The Village," Goldin went on, "must be exciting. Not for me, but I guess it must be exciting."

"I wouldn't know."

"Huh?"

"I wouldn't know," the girl repeated simply. "I've never been here before."

There was something about the delivery of the line which

a proper mixture of cold and hot was hard to come by. She settled for a stream of water that was much hotter than she normally preferred. The butt end of a bar of soap remained in the soap dish and she lathered herself furiously with it, rubbing the soap into her white skin and rinsing herself until her skin squeaked with cleanliness. She spent a long time under the stream of water, washing every trace of the bus trip from her system, then stepped out onto a postage stamp bath mat and rubbed herself dry with a huge orange towel.

When she left the bathroom, she almost keeled over. The bathroom had been like a steam bath and the sudden switch in temperature weakened her. She walked very unsteadily to the bedroom, sat down heavily on the bed, then slipped between the sheets and settled her head on a soft pillow.

She thought about the job, wondered whether she should cut her hair so that she might look more like a New Yorker, thought about prints she would buy for the walls and a rug she would buy for the floor in the living room. She thought also about money—she had almost five hundred dollars in her suitcase, part in travelers checks and part in cash, which should make things easier for her. Monday, during her lunch hour, she would have to find a bank and open a checking account. In the meantime there were plenty of other things to do—shopping, especially. The refrigerator in the kitchenette was a small one but it would have to do. She would fill it with food, lay in a supply of pots and pans and dishes and knives and forks and spoons. It would be cheaper if she ate at home. And when a job paid a miraculous fifty dollars a week, with a ten-dollar raise due at the end of two months, and when your apartment set you back a cool hundred a month, saving money was important.

She thought about these things and she thought about other things, memories mostly, both of Clifton and of Schwernersville. Some of the memories were pleasant and others were not. Her mind took them in turn, lazily, and then her mind drifted on gently.

And she slept.

While Joyce Kendall slept and dreamed private dreams, the tenants of the apartment directly above her, the front apartment on the third floor of 21 Gay Street, Jean Fitzgerald and Terri Leigh, were drinking their dinner.

Dinner that night was primarily gin. While Terri relaxed on the sofa and listened to a Bartok string quartet, Jean combined gin, Italian vermouth and ice in a plastic cocktail shaker and shook the mixture diligently. The vermouth was something of an afterthought. The brew was seven parts gin to one part vermouth because, as Jean maintained, if you are going to drink gin you don't want to louse it up by pouring wine into it. When the shaking process had accomplished the twin feats of cooling the mixture and hiding the vermouth, Jean located two cocktail glasses in the kitchen cupboard, brought them into the living room and filled them with the liquid. Into each she dropped two pickled onions.

"Voila," she said. "Gibsons. Made by a master. Michael's Pub could do no better."

Terri nodded solemnly. They clinked glasses and drank. Then Jean refilled the glasses and the process was repeated.

Jean was 25 and Terri was 22. Jean was a brunette and Terri was a blonde. Jean's dark brown hair was cropped close to her head in an Italian-style haircut and Terri's yellow hair fell almost to her waist. Jean was a secretary to an advertising director and Terri modelled part-time for Village artists. Jean had a long, lean figure, looked good in slacks and wore lipstick sparingly. Terri was built for comfort, looked good in sweaters, and wore too much makeup.

Jean was a lesbian and so was Terri.

They had been living together for almost a year, going together to gay parties, drinking a little too much at the parties, in lesbian bars, or in the happy privacy of their own apartment and making gentle or violent love in the huge double bed they shared. Jean had never slept with a man and never wanted to. Terri had slept with several and had never enjoyed it.

Now Jean sat in a straight-backed chair and Terri lounged on the couch. The Bartok record finished and a Randy Weston record dropped on top of it. The piano music was hard and driving and, at the same time, extremely intimate. Glasses clinked. Gin disappeared.

"Hard day?"

"Terrible," Jean said. "Hotter than hell."

"At least your office is air-conditioned."

"The subway isn't air-conditioned. Neither are the streets. Neither are the people who breathe on you, especially the mealy little men who pinch your behind in the subway. God, I hate men who pinch! I stepped on one of them today. Ground my heel into his instep. Hurt him like mad but he was too ashamed of himself to yell."

Terri giggled.

"Besides," Jean went on, "air-conditioning is limited. This apartment is air-conditioned. And it's still too goddamned hot for me to be comfortable."

"Maybe you're overdressed."

Jean grinned. "Could be," she said. She started to set her glass down on the coffee table, then changed her mind and drained it. Then she put it down and stood up, unbuttoning her blouse as she rose. The blouse was light green silk. She took it off and threw it to the floor.

"You like?"

"Yummy."

"Still too warm."

The bra followed the blouse. Jean Fitzgerald's breasts were small and went well with the long-limbed, boyish look of her. They were well-shaped and firm. The nipples were tiny rubies set in blonde marble.

"You like?"

"Mmmmmmm."

"But still too warm."

Jean undressed with deliberate slowness, doing a gentle strip-tease to the pulsating jazz on the record player. She let her clothing fall to the floor and ignored it, standing nude and proud in the middle of the living-room floor.

"Ummmmm."

"Now you're the one who's overdressed."

"Also lazy. Come help me."

Jean walked slowly to the couch, sat beside Terri, reached for her. The blonde girl giggled as hands raced over the front of her blouse, found the buttons and opened them. Jean's fingers were deft with the buttons and clumsy when they wanted to be clumsy, brushing against Terri's full breasts, teasing the blonde girl into a weird sort of excitement.

"Now take off my bra."

"My, you are lazy, aren't you?"

"Very lazy. Help me."

"Can't even take off your own bra."

"Uh-huh."

"Well—"

Jean reached around Terri's body, straining for the clasp of the bra. Her own bare breasts were drawn up against Terri's chest and her lips touched Terri's throat and left a kiss there. Then the bra was off and cast aside. The blonde's breasts were very large, over-sized, but no less perfect than those of the brunette. Suddenly Jean hugged Terri hard, kissing her at the same time, and the two pairs of breasts were pressed tight together.

The effect was electrical. Simultaneously both girls drew in their breath sharply, then pushed themselves apart. Jean's eyes were glazed and Terri's face was flushed.

"Hey! Go easy, girl."

"Not my fault. You did it. Besides, you have to undress me first. Then we can do it."

"Do what?"

"Guess."

"You don't mean to say a cute little girl like you would want to—"

"Damned right I would."

Jean grinned. She reached for Terri again, and this time her fingers found the button and then the zipper on Terri's red Bermuda shorts. She unbuttoned and unzipped, removed the shorts, leaving the blonde in a pair of wispy panties, which didn't last long.

"Now," she said. "Isn't that cooler?"

"Whee! Feel the breeze!"

"There are better things to feel."

"So feel them."

"Like this?"

"That's the idea."

"And this?"

"That, too, is the idea. I mean, I, uh—"

"Oh, good. Terri's getting excited. Aren't you?"

"Uh—"

Jean's hand's cupped Terri's breasts, squeezing, stroking, touching. Slowly the blonde girl fell back on the couch, her long legs stretched out in front of her, her arms thrown back over her head. Her eyes were closed and there was an expression of complete and total abandon upon her face.

Jean's hands, Jean's hot aggressive hands, were everywhere. They fondled the very soft skin on the underside of Terri's breasts, then found the even softer, impossibly smooth silk-skin of Terri's thighs. Jean's fingers played desperate little games with Terri's breasts, stirring both girls to a hot animal desire.

Jean's mouth, a small mouth, an almost dainty mouth, began to search out the secret places in Terri's perfect body. They kissed, a long and deep kiss of mouth on mouth with tongues probing and searching and bodies pressed tightly together, breasts against breasts, belly against belly. Then Jean's mouth moved lower, to Terri's throat, to Terri's breasts, and Jean's tongue flicked out like fire, licking, stroking, searching.

Terri couldn't stay still any longer. Her whole body burned, itched, ached. Her arms fastened around Jean, holding the dark-haired girl, touching her where Terri knew she wanted to be touched.

And passion mounted.

"My darling—"

"Hush. Kiss me."

"I need you so much, baby."

"And I need you—"

Words of love and gestures to match them. Hands going everywhere and touching everything, hands on breasts and bellies and buttocks and thighs, lips and tongues joining hands, desire blazing and racing and growing and churning.

Lovemaking.

The world turning, pitching, rising. The earth churning, boiling. Sweat gluing two bodies together, sweat and heat and love.

Tension and more tension. Fury and more fury and, impossibly, more fury.

The peak. Reached, surmounted.

Peace.

Voices, soft, gentle, coming through a filter.

"It was good, wasn't it?"

"Divine, darling."

"It always is for us, isn't it?"

"Every time."

"I love you, Jean. You know I love you, don't you? You know how much I love you."

"Of course I do. And I love you, baby."

Near-silence. A clock ticking in the bedroom. Auto noises rising from the streets like smoke. People talking in the distance. The clatter of a typewriter in another apartment. Silence, or the next thing to it.

"We have so much, Jean."

"So very much."

"And we'll always have it. Forever, Jean."

"Forever, my baby."

"Because I love you."

"And I love you."

"And we'll always be together and it'll always be like this. Even when we're sixty."

"Even when we're nine years older than that."

Laughter.

"More, Jean. I need you again."

"Baby—"

Bodies reaching for each other. Passion like a furnace. More perspiration and more small animal noises.

And more love.

CHAPTER 2

While Joyce Kendall slept in apartment 2-A, and while Terri Leigh and Jean Fitzgerald made love in apartment 3-A, Pete Galton in apartment 8-B pounded a portable typewriter and tried to forget a girl named Linda.

Galton was 26, going bald, a nervous chain-smoker with a perpetual five o'clock shadow. A few months ago he had been a reporter and rewrite man for a leading New York daily. A few months ago, for that matter, he had been a part-time bedmate and full-time lover of a girl by the name of Linda Medellin, a pretty little thing with black hair and happy breasts. Had been, that is.

You, he said aloud to himself, *are nothing but a had-been.* That seemed to call for a drink, so he answered the call by taking a liberal swig from a bottle that rested on top of the desk next to the portable typewriter. He would have kept the bottle in the desk drawer but that, he reminded himself, was a standard reporter's gambit, and he was no longer a reporter. Nor was he a rewrite man, nor was he the part-time bedmate or full-time lover of Linda Medellin, girl of the black hair and the happy breasts, goddamn her to eternal hell fire.

Which, in turn, called for another drink.

It was a hell of a note, he told himself, a hell of a note. While the job on the New York *Record* had admittedly been less than the greatest job in the world, it had been a job, and a good job. He had liked the newspaper business and he had especially liked the New York *Record*, in spite of its myriad and occasionally classic faults. True, the *Record* took the bulk of its news copy almost verbatim from a top morning daily. True, the *Record* could have laid it on the line a bit by printing on yellow paper. But at the same time the *Record* was the sole liberal voice in New York, a crusading daily with blood in its eye. Pete had liked it.

Quoth the raven, he thought, *up yours*.

That didn't make much sense, either, but at least it called for another drink. That was something.

He put down the bottle, capped it, and went back to what he was typing. He was working, more or less, on a novel. But it wasn't as though he had quit his job at the *Record* so that he could go to work on a novel. This was part of the stereotype, just as the vision of a reporter getting fired for drinking was part of the same stereotype. Neither notion happened to fit the case of Pete Galton. The case of Pete Galton was a unique one, and in order to understand it one has to understand what may be called l'affaire Medellin.

Pete had expected to marry Linda Medellin. They went for long walks together and had long talks together and made more than competent love together. Linda was a Brooklyn girl, a graduate of Brooklyn college, currently employed as some sort of minor flunkey in the midtown offices of a mammoth insurance company. They saw each other four or five times a week. At the conclusion of each evening Linda went home to Mama in Brooklyn and Pete came back alone on the Brighton line of the BMT. Sometimes the early part of the evening included a stop at 21 Gay

Street for a happy roll in the happy hay, which pleased both of them tremendously. Not always, however, because the relationship they enjoyed was more than mere sex. Besides, as Pete always thought, they had plenty of time, because, after all, they were going to get married and live in a house in Connecticut with three daughters, all of them blondes with long hair.

It did not work out that way.

Linda, for some reason incomprehensible to Pete, had suddenly gotten married.

Not to Pete.

To somebody else.

And Pete, just as suddenly, was left Linda-less. It was a traumatic experience in the fullest sense of the word and hard-boiled newspaperman or no, Pete had cracked up.

It suddenly seemed extremely unimportant to become the Golden Boy of the New York *Record*, and dreams of Washington correspondentships, Pulitzer Prizes and City Desks faded at once from his vision. He started failing to show up at the *Record* at all, until finally, in the interest of fair play, he informed them that he was no longer working for them. They wanted to know why, asked if something was wrong, told him how much they wanted him back, offered a leave of absence and generally attempted to return him to the happy liberal fold. But Pete begged out. He wanted to cut the strings completely, to go all the way out on his own hook, to let things happen for once instead of trying to make them happen.

Which may in some part explain why he was sitting in his apartment that evening, drinking bourbon intermittently and pounding a portable typewriter, also intermittently, and thinking unhappy thoughts about Linda.

The book he was writing seemed to be coming along fairly well, though it was hard to tell. It was the first book he had ever written, for one thing. He'd done some freelance writing in the past outside of his newspaper work, some true crime stuff for the fact-detective magazines while he was on the police beat in Brooklyn, an occasional historical piece for the men's adventure mags, a few short stories that had never sold any place. This was different.

For one thing, it wasn't aimed anywhere in particular. It was just going along, a slow-paced low-keyed story about a guy not particularly unlike Pete Galton, a book that moved along a page or so at a time, with no outline, no plot held firmly in his mind, no big message, no particular notion. It was just a book.

The working title was *Song of Experience*, a reference to the poetry of William Blake. That was all he had so far—a title, an opening quote and around thirty pages of copy. He didn't know when the book would be finished or how long it would run. He didn't want to be finished, for that matter. When the book was done he wouldn't have anything to do with himself.

Not that he did much now. He had enough money set aside—savings from his job which had paid quite well, plus a tiny inheritance that he had never gotten around to spending. It had been over three weeks since he had left the *Record* and there still seemed to be plenty of money on hand. He didn't spend much. His life was simple and inexpensive. He got out of bed at eleven or so, scrambled a pair of eggs, browned a few link sausages, and washed the meal down with a jolt of instant coffee. Then he would go out for a walk, wandering rather aimlessly around the Village, enjoying the relaxed pressureless atmosphere of Greenwich Village in June. His walk usually wound up in Washington Square Park, where he sat on a bench and smoked, talking to people some of the time, watching people the rest of the time, watching and listening, and thinking his own thoughts.

He would have dinner out, a hero sandwich on Macdougal Street, a plate of fish and chips at the Brittania on Sullivan, an Italian meal at the Grand Ticino or Joe's. Then a few beers at the Kettle, then more walking. If he ran into somebody or if there was something of interest going on, that took up the evening. Otherwise, he went home, stopping at a liquor store on Seventh Avenue for a pint of bourbon. Then he stationed himself with bourbon and typewriter, knocking off a page or two and punching a hole in the pint.

The writing was tougher now. For one thing, bourbon had a way of making his fingers hit the wrong keys. For another, there was an outside force which was disturbing his composure. The outside force consisted of the pair of girls in 3-A.

Damned little dykes, he thought. *I don't mind how frequently you make it, but you could at least have the decency to make it quietly.*

He listened to the squeaking of the couch and he remembered what the girls next door looked like and he imagined how they must look at that particular moment, lying naked in each other's arms and finding cute little things to do to each other. The thought made writing out of the question. He limped to the bottom of the page, then took the sheet of paper from the typewriter and added it to the stack of completed manuscript pages. He was too dragged to do any more writing. It was, he reasoned, the fault of the dykes. By a single couch-squeal they had accomplished three things—they had made him realize how much he needed a woman, and how alone he was, and what a prison the apartment was becoming.

Pete Galton stood up, returned the typewriter to its carrying case, and placed it in the closet to discourage burglars. He sipped once more at the bourbon, leaving enough in the bottle to take the edge off the morning after. Then, thoughtfully, he placed the bottle by the side of his bed. That way he would be able to reach it without so much as opening his eyes.

On hot days like this one he generally wrote in his under-shorts. Writing in your undershorts is acceptable anywhere, but going out on the street in them is out of the question, even in the relatively liberal atmosphere of Greenwich Village. He got dressed—a blue shirt with the sleeves permanently rolled up and a pair of light-weight summer slacks—and left the apartment, locking the door behind him. On his way out he growled angri-ly at the closed door of the apartment where the couch was still squeaking in a rhythm as old as the human race itself.

It was almost as warm on the street as it had been in his apart-ment. He stood in front of 21 Gay Street for a moment, not sure where to go. He wanted something to happen, something fast and furious with nothing coming behind it, a quick sexual outlet with no strings attached, no hangover, no claims.

He walked from Gay Street to Christopher, over Christopher to Bedford, until he found the place he was looking for. It was a cellar bar on Bedford Street, a place you only found if you were looking for it very carefully. Tourists never found it and most

Villagers were unaware of its existence. Not even it's name, *Ariadne's Web*, appeared anywhere outside.

It was an unprepossessing place. The walls had been painted flat black in the twenties and left untouched since then. The heavy oak tables were the same as they had been many years ago. And the men and women, sitting and staring into wine glasses like absinthe drinkers, looked as though they had been there for years, and as though they would remain motionless until the end of time.

Pete found a table. He ordered a glass of red wine from the bearded waiter and paid for it when it arrived. It was sour but delicious, and he sipped it slowly, wondering how it would mix with the bourbon. Poorly, he decided.

Pete glanced around the room. In one corner a boy of about eighteen slumped in his chair, head thrown back, eyes fixed, staring at the lightbulb that dangled from the ceiling. The boy's pupils were little black dots and his nostrils were distended. His fingers drummed a rigid tattoo on the tabletop.

Cocaine.

A few men and women whom Pete sized up quickly as heroin addicts sat immutable, occasionally raising a heavy hand to scratch a chest, their eyes opening and closing in remarkably slow blinks, their breathing shallow. They were waiting patiently for the Man, the Connection who would make everything good again.

Pete drank his wine. *Get in deep*, he thought. *Be the world's greatest spectator. Watch human sickness through a neat knothole and if you ask me I could write a book. What else?*

The waiter came around again and Pete ordered another glass

of wine. He drank half of it and discovered that he was a little bit drunk. The discovery was not at all unpleasant.

The front door swung open. Heads turned—junkies waiting for the Man wheeled around to see if it was Him. They saw a girl instead, sighed, turned back and waited once more. Pete Galton stared at the girl and watched her walk to a table.

He looked at her, appraised her and decided that this was the one, this would do for the evening, it would be quick and easy and good enough for a night, with no strings attached and no hangover, no heartaches on either side, no nothing, nothing but quick relief and quick abandon.

Which was enough.

She was not beautiful, but she did not have to be beautiful. She was young, maybe too young, maybe under eighteen—God, were there girls left in the world under eighteen?—but she was there and she didn't look like a junkie. She knew what was happening and she wouldn't mind if it happened to her. She had dirty blonde hair and she wore it in a pony tail. Her eyes were eye-shadowed, her lips gummed up with white lipstick. Beat? That was this year's classification. And what would next year's classification be? And did anybody care?

He walked over to her, taking the remaining half-glass of wine with him. She looked up and studied him, saying nothing, her face expressionless. He sat down without waiting for an invitation, raised the glass of wine in a mock toast, and drained it.

"What's your scene, man?"

Her voice was low, disinterested. He didn't answer her. Instead, he stared into her eyes. There was no worry, he decided. She was over eighteen.

"I want to make it with you," he said finally. He grinned inwardly at the way he shifted gears automatically, talking hip talk now as if it were his native language. "I want to take you to my pad," he went on, "and tear your clothes off and toss you on the bed and play games with you."

She looked at him. "I don't hustle," she said.

"Crazy. I don't have eyes to pay."

"Maybe I have no eyes to play. You come on strong, baby. What are you on?"

"I swing with my own thoughts."

"Crazy thoughts," she said. "You got a name, baby?"

"Pete," he said.

"Crazy name. Dig, I don't hustle. I just told you, I don't hustle."

"I'm hip."

"So—"

"Like we'll make it for the sheer hell of it."

She thought that one over. He stared at her breasts and his desire for her began to turn into a physical thing, strong and demanding. It was too warm to be cool.

"Pete—"

He looked up.

"First, like I never have eyes to make it straight. When I make it I like to make it on pot. You dig pot?"

"Sometimes."

"It makes everything cooler," she said. "Deeper. You hear the notes and the space between the notes. But," she explained, "I'm out."

"Out?"

"No pot. If you got the bread for a ball, I got a connection."

"How much?"

"A nickel'll swing it."

A nickel, he knew, meant five dollars. He had five dollars. He nodded absently.

"There's another thing."

"What?"

She shrugged. "I like . . . have my own kind of kicks. You might not have eyes for them."

"I'll play."

"You sure?"

"I'm sure."

"Like there's one thing you got to do to me first or I won't be able to cook. You know what I mean?"

He nodded.

"You willing?"

"Sure."

She smiled. "Groovy," she said. "Hit me with a nickel. Then wait here while I cop. I'll be back in like five, ten minutes."

He took out his wallet, gave her a five dollar bill and watched her disappear through the door again. She swung her behind when she walked and her dungarees were tight on the swinging behind, which made a pleasant picture. Pete wondered idly whether he would ever see her again, whether his five dollars would disappear with her. It didn't make too much difference but he sort of hoped she would be back. For one thing, he wanted her. For another, he had never had marijuana before, despite what he had told her. He'd been planning on trying it for months but had never gotten around to it.

He had another glass of wine while he waited. For some reason the wine wasn't reaching him now. A few minutes ago he had felt drunk, and now he was almost sober again. It was strange.

He sipped the wine slowly and waited for her.

She did come back. She walked in, looked at him and looked away quickly, then motioned toward the door. He waited while she looked around the place and left. Then he walked out after her and joined her on the sidewalk.

"I copped," she said. "A nickel's worth. He threw in some paper, too. You know how to wheel?"

He shook his head.

"Then I will. I'm not too good but I can roll something smokable. We'll manage. My name's Sandy, by the way. Where did you say your pad was?"

He showed her. They walked side by side, back over Bedford to Christopher, across Christopher to Gay Street. They did not hold hands or talk, and Pete knew suddenly just how necessary the pot was going to be. Now the whole thing was ridiculous, ludicrous, a man and a girl going to a bedroom with nothing in common but a vague and undirected sexual urge. They would have to get high, he thought, or they simply would not have the slightest inclination to make love. They would have to get high or they would be bored with each other.

He led her into his building and up the stairs to his apartment. He unlocked the door and they walked inside. The apartment— one room plus a miniature kitchen plus a bathroom—was a mess.

There were cigarettes butted on the floor, circles from glasses on the furniture. The bed was unmade.

They sat on the edge of the bed and he watched while she rolled the marijuana cigarettes. The marijuana came in a small brown envelope. She opened it, held a piece of gummed paper between the thumb and forefinger of her left hand, spilled a little of the green-brown stuff into the paper and rolled a cigarette. She rolled it very thin and twisted the ends. She made six cigarettes, then closed the envelope.

"Now we swing, Pete."

He knew how to smoke it. He took one of the cigarettes and put it in his mouth, then lit it with a match. He sucked the smoke straight into his lungs in a long drag, keeping his lips slightly parted. The smoke was hot and burned the back of his throat. The taste was hard to describe—not bitter, not sweet, very distinctive.

He passed her the cigarette, holding his breath until she had done the same thing and was passing the cigarette back to him. Then he let the smoke out in a rush and took another drag on the cigarette. This time he didn't notice the heat of the smoke as much as before.

"You feeling anything?"

He shrugged. He was patient, awaiting the reaction that he was certain would come.

"You got to help it along," she was saying. "Relax, try to feel it moving inside of you. Like it's music and you're trying hard to listen to it. Like tuning in on it."

They smoked. His arms grew loose, heavy, and he could feel the blood in his veins, the movements of his internal organs.

Things moved very slowly, very slowly, and he could see with his eyes closed and hear without listening.

"You're getting there, baby." It was Sandy's voice but it seemed to be coming from a hundred miles away, filtering slowly through to him. "You're going way up, baby. We're both flying. You get that, baby? Flying!"

She started giggling and he couldn't understand what was so funny. Then, unaccountably, he was laughing too, giggling hysterically over nothing at all. He couldn't control himself, just kept laughing and laughing like a lunatic.

They smoked, laughed, talked and said nothing. Then all at once the marijuana was gone and they were sitting side by side on the bed, looking very intently at each other, and Pete knew that it was going to happen, that in its own way it was going to be very good, that he needed it now more than ever.

It wasn't that pot was a stimulant, he thought to himself. His sex urge was no greater than it had been before. It was just the way the drug had of making all the connections, of showing you the spaces between the notes. Wasn't that how she had put it? Something along those lines.

"Come here, baby."

They did not know each other, and did not particularly like each other, and under other circumstances kissing would have been ridiculous. But they did kiss, now, and it was good—a sensual kiss, with his tongue plunging deep into the confines of her mouth, tasting the sweet taste of her, tasting the un-bitter, un-sweet taste of the marijuana, tasting and caressing.

A long kiss.

She was wearing a white jersey tee-shirt that he pulled over her head and dropped to the floor. She was not wearing a brassiere. Her breasts were big and soft, nothing like the pert happy breasts of Linda, but now Sandy's breasts seemed eminently desirable. He cupped one in the palm of his hand, closing his eyes and feeling the softness and smoothness of the breast. He could see it through closed eyelids, see it and feel it and—

They took off their clothes. He kissed her on the mouth again, then crouched over her and began kissing her breasts. Taste, touch, smell—all sensations were magnified incredibly and he found himself wanting her urgently, needing to take her and possess her at once.

He reached for her, aching for her, and she drew away.

"Baby, you promised!"

He looked at her, unable to understand what she was talking about. What on earth had he promised?

"Like what you would do," she explained. "Before we make it there's something you have to do."

He remembered now, very vaguely. Then she showed him what she wanted him to do, and he did it the way she wanted him to do it.

And she moaned.

The caress set her on fire. She writhed and squirmed and moaned and she was ready and it began. Their lovemaking—except that it was not lovemaking, not by any stretch of the imagination. It was valuable and it was necessary, but it was not lovemaking and could never be called anything of the sort.

Because love had nothing to do with it.

It was furious yet lacking in fury, intense yet curiously detached, profound yet meaningless. It was a new experience, a new batch of sensations, a brand-new and totally different approach to the same old thing. He felt everything, everything there was to feel, and yet in the depth of his being he felt absolutely nothing at all.

In a strictly physical sense it was better than anything that had preceded it. It lasted longer, for one thing. Time lost all importance—there was only him and the woman, only what they were doing, removed from the world in space and time. There were moans and groans, twists and thrusts, hands on flesh and mouth on mouth. That was all. Time and space were unknown quantities, pointless decimals lost in a void of smoke.

But in any sense other than the physical, in any frame of reference other than the purely sensual, there was nothing happening, nothing going on, nothing at all. There was no rapport, no feeling, no meaning, no depth.

Which was strange. Very strange and very hard to comprehend in its totality. Better to ignore the missing depth, the missing meaning. Better to explore the physical, to feel anything and everything, to make an eternity last forever.

Higher.

To a peak—or was it a plateau, a mesa, a level foothill?

To a peak . . . of sorts. And peace.

They were lying on the bed. Their bodies were not touching and their eyes were closed.

"Baby?"

"Yeah?"

"Let's like fall asleep, Pete. It's good, falling asleep while you're still a little bit high. You get a good sleep that way. Two or three hours and you get as much rest as a night of straight sleep. It's good that way."

"Okay."

Silence for a while.

"Pete?"

"Mmmmm—"

"That was a gas, Pete. Tell me something. You never made pot before, did you?"

No answer.

"I'm not putting you down. I just wanted to know. Dig, I'll be gone when you wake up."

"Huh?"

"Like I'll go home. You'll probably want to be rid of me by then anyhow. You ever want to connect with me, I hang around Ariadne's Web a lot of the time. Or the Fishhook. That's over on the east side off Cooper Square."

"I know the place."

"It's a good place. But listen—I'm leaving the rest of the pot here. I mean, you paid for it. And we only used maybe a quarter of it. It'll last you a while. You want to cop, I can always put you hip to a good connection. Just get in touch with me."

"Fine."

"I'm going to sleep now."

She stopped talking and he let himself drift off in the general direction of sleep. He was still very high, although the full force of the marijuana had been dissipated slightly by the sexual activity. He was still high enough for his mind to follow strange and unfamiliar thought-patterns, racing along over strange trails and hitting weird resting-places.

He didn't fight it. He relaxed and let himself think about Sandy. He wondered who she was and where she had come from and what she did and where she lived and what her last name was. He felt as though he was having a glimpse of a new world, or as if he was looking at the same old world through somewhat different eyes.

A strange night.

He wondered vaguely what was coming up next. More of the same? Or a retreat, a trip back to the relative safety of a job on the *Record*, stories to write and people to see and a steady seventy-five hundred a year, then a wife and kids and a happy happy home in Connecticut or Nassau County or—

The thoughts trailed away and he watched a parade of colored lights across the retina of his mind. He thought about Sandy and the two dykes next door and Linda and the girl who had just moved in that night—he had caught a glimpse of her but couldn't remember what she looked like.

Then he thought about nothing at all, merely watching the mental lights, eyes closed. Sandy slept at his side but he was not conscious of her now, had, in fact, already forgotten her. He watched the colored lights, watched them glimmer and twinkle, and finally watched them fade slowly, very slowly, to blackness.

He slept very deeply and very well.

CHAPTER 3

Joyce Kendall was watching the clock.

Watching the clock is a bad habit, even when you have held a job so long that it has become the penultimate in boredom, the quintessence of routine. When you are watching the clock on the third day of a new job, watching it with bated breath, this hardly bodes well for the future.

The clock informed Joyce that in ten minutes it would be five o'clock and she could get the merry hell away from the offices of Armageddon Publications, Inc. That, she decided, was fortunate. More than ten minutes would have been tough to take.

The job had been a mistake. To begin with, its title was appallingly misleading. She had been given to understand that she was to function as a first reader, the first eye to pore over the carefully typed manuscripts of aspiring authors eager for success. While the notion of poring over the tripe that Armageddon published wasn't all that exciting to begin with, it was at least a "creative" job, an entry into the exciting world of publishing. Bad enough, but better than what she wound up doing.

What she wound up doing was a little frightening. She was, to all intents and purposes, a typist. She spent her eight hours—minus an hour for lunch and the standard number of coffee breaks and trips to the water cooler—pounding out miscellaneous trivia.

Letters, order forms, trivial twaddle. Playing jockey to an ancient Underwood was her idea of nothing to do, but that was also her job.

The "first reader" bit came into play, but hardly in the way she had expected. For one thing, manuscripts submitted by anybody remotely worthwhile went straight past her desk without bothering to stop and chat. If an author had ever sold anything to Armageddon Publications, or if he was known at all by anybody, he did not need the approval of the first reader. If he was represented by a competent agent—and, it seemed, all good authors were—he also missed the indignity of a preliminary examination by one Joyce Kendall.

If, on the other hand, he was an incompetent, then he fell into Joyce's hands. And there were many incompetents, one less competent than the next.

Unknown manuscripts were relegated to what was known as the slush pile, and it was there that Joyce came into the picture. She spent twenty minutes to a half hour of each working day slitting open the brown manila envelopes, reading the proffered trash within, and then doing one of two things with it. Either she returned it posthaste in the enclosed stamped self-addressed envelope with a printed rejection slip or she passed it on to a second reader. In three days she had glanced over approximately one hundred fifty pieces of garbage and had returned one hundred forty-eight to their hopeful authors. The other two scripts—one a confession story submitted to Armageddon's two confession magazines, *Desperate Love Stories* and *Passionate Confessions*, the other, a true-adventure piece aimed at *True Male Tales* and entitled something along the lines of *I Banged A Boa Constrictor*—had been passed on, and Joyce neither knew nor cared what would become of them. She knew only that the whole routine was impossible, that she was a typist being paid off in glamour that didn't happen to exist, and that the job was unbearable.

Five to five. She fussed with her hair, applied lipstick, and scanned the room, watching the other girls who were toiling right up to the bell like good earnest wage-slaves, covered her typewriter, straightened up her desk, and waited.

Then it was five o'clock, and she left.

The job was a disappointment, and, for that matter, so was New York. There was an excitement about the town that she could not deny, but this excitement was more than counter-balanced by the fact that she was left completely out of it. In only five days in the city she had managed to settle haphazardly into a rut. There was the job, the subway to and home from work, the apartment, the Gristede's where she shopped for food, the newsstand where she bought the *Times* every morning and the *Record* every night, and there were the Village streets she wandered occasionally. The Village streets were admittedly lively and intense, but again it was a life and an intensity which left her out in the cold.

She was alone—and lonely.

Very lonely.

There was little to compare with loneliness in a huge city. It was unlike anything she had ever experienced, although her life had frequently been a lonely one, and it was something she did not enjoy in the least. Loneliness had a way of sapping your existence of vitality, of meaning, of reducing everything to nothing at all.

There was the morning—a day or two ago—when she had

awakened to the jangle of the alarm clock and turned her face wearily from the pillow, her eyes coming open slowly. She scrambled out of the bed, reached the clock, managed to turn it off, and then fell headlong upon the bed once more.

Sleep began to crowd in on her and it would have been pleasant to surrender to it. But she fought with sleep, remembering that she had to get to work. And she definitely had to get to work, because, she realized all at once, the people at her office were the only people in New York who knew that she was alive, the only people who could look at her and recognize her.

A frightening thought.

So she had showered, dressed, headed for the yawning mouth of the subway that spat her out in the middle of morning Manhattan, and found her way to the offices of Armageddon Publications. And there, safe once more in the loneliness of a crowd, she realized that not even the people at work really knew or wanted to know her.

No one did.

She was a girl who had never had many close friends, but this genuine loneliness was something she had never experienced and was thoroughly unprepared for. Schwernersville had been a small town, horrible in the way that Midwestern small towns can be horrible, narrow and Babbitish and stupid, but when she walked down the Main Street of Schwernersville people recognized her, said hello to her, stopped to talk to her.

Clifton had been still smaller, a tiny liberal arts college devoid of privacy, and while she had led a quiet life there, she had never had a chance at the complete solitude afforded by the nation's greatest city. There were always people—a roommate, classmates, boys who took her to movies and parties and who attempted to seduce her in parked cars. Boys with hungry hands and moist mouths, boys who wanted her and who didn't try to hide their desire. Boys who tried to seduce her, and a few who succeeded.

Not many had succeeded. Just two, really—Joe Cardigan and Ron Gibbs. And the two had been very different. Joe was a love affair, a very intense and very painful love affair that began in the fall of her junior year and carried through until spring. Joe was tall, lean, tense, a history major with a sharp tongue and a fast mind. She had been violently attracted to him, and the combination of his attractiveness and skilled approach and her own questioning seeking need for sex had permitted him to succeed where others had failed.

The first time—a parked car, late at night, a little too much wine, Joe's hands more demanding than before, Joe's caresses infinitely more effective, her own resistance low. Clothing half-off, half-on, the painfully awkward move from front seat to back, the fumbling that in itself increased passion rather than dissipating it. And then the pain, harsh and searing, and wondering what to do, how to do it, because none of the books actually told you how to make love and it was confusing, painful, embarrassing.

And then the knowledge that was born in the blood, and her own body making the right movements all by itself, learning, playing by ear, awkward at first and then graceful in its own awkwardness, with her passion rising incredibly, surprising her, frightening her and then burying the fright forever.

A trip to heaven that ended inches away from fulfillment. But pleasure, amazing pleasure that was good, very good.

And two nights later, in a real bed in a motel, with the

combined guilt and excitement of registering as man and wife, and slow, complete undressing, and a coming together that was slow and gentle and, for the first time, complete. This time they built their pleasure slowly and firmly together, climbing together, working together, with his hands on her breasts and his mouth glued to her mouth, and the world racing and time miraculously suspended.

And fulfillment now, perfect and almost everlasting.

After that they were together constantly, sleeping together, walking together, talking together. Their relationship was not one in which permanence was a spoken word. Marriage was something off in the distance, something to be thought of privately but never to be discussed. They lived for the moment. The moments were good, perfect.

The end came in April.

It was a strange ending. What it boiled down to, she knew, was that they simply were not right for each other, that no marriage between them could ever work out, that their interests were similar but their personalities had subtle yet basic differences that made a lasting relationship altogether out of the question. Thus it had to end, and when the ending came it should not have been a surprise. But it was.

There were little strains that developed over a two-month period. Then there was a fight that depressed both of them and left them more or less unable to talk to one another. They simply had nothing to say, no way of communicating.

There was the inevitable reconciliation, the lovemaking accompanying it that was born of desperation and conceived in misery. And then the inevitable reconciliation was superseded by the equally inevitable break-up, the final break-up, and that was the end of it. After that they never spoke, because speech was impossible between them, because the intimacy they had shared previously was embarrassing and made them awkward and ill at ease with each other.

Then, in May, there was Ronald Gibbs. Ron Gibbs was a purgative, a release, a respite from loneliness and an antidote for Joe Cardigan. Ron Gibbs was taken once, taken as directed, a single night in a single motel room, a night of sex, pure and simple, ending forever when the sun came up.

Then there was graduation for both Gibbs and Cardigan, and a trip back to Schwernersville for Joyce Kendall, and then in the fall the return for the final year at Clifton. And then there were no more affairs, few dates, her own graduation, the trip to New York, and more loneliness of a new and different kind. Five days of it, a short time, but painful because there seemed to be little if any prospect of the loneliness ever ending. It would stretch on, and the job would stretch on, and where would it end? It wouldn't end. Or it would—and she would go back to Schwernersville, her suitcase in hand, her mouth thin and lifeless, looking for something. For what? A man and 2.7 children and a white house with green shutters and a fence around it—to keep out the world.

Her loneliness was strangely asexual. A hunger for sex is easily assuaged, especially if the hungry one is an attractive woman. Such a woman has no difficulty finding a man willing to make love to her. Joyce knew that she would have no problem in that respect, there were always men who would be willing, and even in New York she had already noticed through her loneliness that there were men who stared at her on street corners, men in the office who would respond gleefully if given the least encouragement. But she didn't want sex, not especially, not as a purgative or a crutch or anything of the sort. She wanted somebody to talk to.

The subway disgorged her at 4th Street and she hurried up the stairway, heading for home. Home? Not home. The apartment, then. 21 Gay Street. Home.

The day was warm and muggy, the sky overcast, and she was lonelier than ever. She decided all at once to start a conversation with somebody, somebody who lived in her building, man or woman, it didn't matter, whoever happened to be the first person she saw.

She got to her building but she didn't go inside. Instead, she sat on the stoop, waiting. Waiting for somebody. Anybody. Anybody at all.

A man was the first one, a man between twenty-five and thirty, with two day's growth of beard on his face and a weary look in his eyes. He walked up to the building with the distinctive gait of someone who was drunk but not drunk enough to stagger. It was Pete Galton.

She looked at him, scared for a moment to approach him, then remembered her resolution and stood suddenly, her eyes on him. After all, she had made up her mind, she had planned, and she always carried through with her plans, always, whether or not she wanted to. It was the way she was.

He looked at her and the expression in his eyes was not one she could identify. There was something strange about him and she was lost for a moment, unable to say anything.

Then she smiled, a forced smile, and said: "My name is Joyce Kendall. I live in this building."

He simply stared at her.

"I'm from Iowa," she added.

He looked at her, opened his mouth, then closed it.

"I just wanted to say hello."

His voice was low and surly. "Congratulations," he said. "Why don't you find somebody else to say hello to?"

Her eyes went wide.

"Go back to Iowa," he advised her. "Go find a house to haunt. Just so you leave me alone."

She stepped back without thinking and he walked past her, opened the door with his key and disappeared into the building. She watched until he had disappeared, then again sat down on the stoop, staring out across the street and seeing nothing at all. Obviously she had said something wrong, but what it was that had so thoroughly annoyed him was impossible for her to determine. What could it have been? She was pleasant and decent enough. She wasn't a girl on the make, a tramp or anything of the sort, and he should have been able to figure that out. He was drunk, of course, she could tell that much, but he wasn't so drunk that he didn't know what he was doing. At least he didn't look that drunk. Then why had he snapped at her?

Maybe he was just a peculiarly obnoxious man. Or maybe he was suspicious of any woman who talked to a strange man. Maybe he thought she was a nymphomaniac, or a prostitute with a unique come-on, or something along those lines. That didn't seem sensible, but neither did anything else. It was the only rationalization that occurred to her.

She wanted to cry for some unaccountable reason, and she wanted to take his advice and go back to Schwernersville, where people were friendly even if they were dull and narrow. She wanted to go far from New York, far from 21 Gay Street, far from Greenwich Village, very far from the unshaven man with the low voice and the unpleasant words.

But she did not move. She waited.

Then a girl approached, an attractive girl, and Joyce decided to try again. Perhaps it would be easier with a girl. There would be no chance of a sexual misinterpretation, nothing but casual friendship suggested by her approach. It would be safer with a girl and easier.

The girl was tall, slender, pretty, with dark hair cut short and a good figure and pretty eyes. Again Joyce stood up, forcing a smile. The girl stopped.

"I live here," Joyce said, "and my name is Joyce Kendall and I just moved to New York and I'm terribly lonely and I just wanted to say hello. If you don't mind."

"Goodness. No, of course I don't mind."

"Do you live here?"

"That's right. You must have just moved into 2-A. I live right above you. You must be pretty lonely."

"I am."

"Don't you know anybody in New York?"

"Not a soul."

"Working?"

"Sort of. I'm a first reader at Armageddon Publications. Sort of a typist with prestige."

The girl laughed, a low and easy laugh. "Poor kid," she said. "Look, you don't have any plans for tonight, do you?"

She shook her head.

"Then come with me," the girl said. "My roommate's a good cook and we'll have plenty for three. You'll like her—she's a nice kid. We'll have a feed and then go out drinking or something. Sound okay to you?"

Joyce brightened. "It sounds . . . fine. If you're sure I won't get in the way. I don't want to put you to any trouble or anything. I mean, I can manage alone if—"

"Hey!" The girl took her arm, the pressure of her fingers simultaneously comforting and disturbing, and led her to the door. "If you'd be getting in the way," she said, "you wouldn't have been invited in the first place. Just relax and come on."

They entered the building and started up the stairs. "I forgot the introduction routine. You said your name was Joyce something-or-other, didn't you?"

"Joyce Kendall."

"Joyce Kendall. That's a nice name, Joyce. My name is Jean. Jean Fitzgerald."

They walked up the stairs. Joyce was not alone any longer.

Jean Fitzgerald didn't know quite what to make of the whole bit. Here was this girl coming on as gay as a jay, obviously looking for somebody to play house with. And yet there was something wrong. A lesbian had to develop a pretty good sense of instinctual judgment if she wanted to stay on her feet, or be swept properly off them, and if there was one thing Jean's instinctual sense told her, it was that Joyce Kendall was *not* gay.

Or, if she was, she didn't know it.

Which confused the issue. Here was a girl, beautiful and eminently desirable, who had introduced herself to a lesbian without seeming to know what she was doing.

Jean was confused.

The problem, she thought, was to figure out where to go. There was an obvious answer. The place to go was upstairs, where Terri was creating dinner. Then the three of them could sit down and eat, playing it properly straight, and if Joyce Kendall was gay she would let something slip, and if she wasn't that would be the end of it. That was obvious.

But there was something else that was almost equally obvious. That was that one Jean Fitzgerald had found herself too strongly attracted to one Joyce Kendall in an altogether too short period of time. Jean had an idea, a not-unpleasant idea, of what it would be like to sleep with Joyce Kendall. She felt the desire building subtly within her, and she wondered just what was going to happen if the girl had no interest in horizontal games, if the girl was straight as an arrow and dumb as a lox.

It might well be frustrating. Damnably frustrating.

They reached the third floor and Jean banged on the apartment door until Terri came and opened it. Looks passed between them, quick looks that sailed over the head of Joyce Kendall. A look from Terri asked what was happening, and an answering look from Jean said simply *Be cool, ask questions later, this one is probably straight and I don't want to tip her yet.* Then, with no loss of momentum, the introductions were made, the small talk was started on its way, and the game began.

The meal was *paella*, a Spanish shrimp-and-rice concoction that Terri created masterfully. Before dinner they had two

Gibsons apiece, drinks that loosened everybody up enough to ease conversation pleasantly but not enough to let cats loose from bags. Joyce talked about college, about New York, about her job, about being lonely, and Jean and Terri remained guarded, cautious, pariahs playing the part of societal pillars.

And all the time Jean's mind raced, imagining, dreaming, planning . . . and remembering.

She remembered one affair, one case of mistaken identification, one very unpleasant experience in her life that she would have liked to forget forever . . .

She had been out of college for a little over a year, living for a little less than a year with a pretty redhead with big breasts and an incredible sexual appetite, a beautiful girl named Lonnie who filled her with pleasure and drove her mad. Lonnie was bisexual, a roommate and lover who would leave her bed and go to a man, a lovely girl who brought everybody pain. Life with Lonnie was hectic and hellish, and life with Lonnie lasted as long as it did and no longer. Then she was alone, not yet firmly introduced to New York's lesbian society and tragically alone.

Then there had been the girl.

A blonde girl, very very young, not more than eighteen, if that, young and fresh and pretty. They had met—at work, over coffee—and they had had dinner together, and Jean had been so strongly attracted to the girl that she couldn't stand it. She had half-known that the girl was not gay, that Jean's hidden meanings sailed past her, that the girl was lost and out of her element. But desire had been the master of reason, or the mistress of reason, and Jean had done something horrible, something she could not yet bear to think about.

Not that first night. Later, two nights later, when the blonde girl named Carole had come to her apartment for dinner and drinks. Skillfully and wretchedly Jean had loaded the drinks, plying the blonde with alcohol until she literally did not know what was happening, literally did not realize what she was doing.

And then it had begun.

It was a game at first. "Pretend I'm a man," Jean had said. "Pretend I'm a man and I'm kissing you. Show me how you would kiss me."

And Jean had taken the blonde girl in her arms and had kissed her, her hot tongue harsh and demanding in Carole's mouth, her arms taut and unyielding. There had been a buried glimmer of understanding in Carole's blue child-eyes, and then the glimmer had faded as the alcohol washed over it.

The trip to the bedroom was accomplished easily enough. Then Jean had removed the girl's clothing, kissing her again, kissing her over and over, exciting the girl until the alcohol and the excitement combined so that the girl was lost forever, lost because Carole did not know that she was with a woman, knew nothing other than that she was receiving pleasure and that the kisses were good and sweet.

Jean had wasted no time. She hated herself, despised herself, but still could not help herself, could not keep her hands from Carole's plump girlish breasts, could not keep from touching and kissing all the sweetness that was Carole.

Jean did everything to the girl, everything that could be done.

Her heart swelled when she saw that the girl enjoyed it as much as she herself did, that her skillful caresses were setting Carole on fire. She showed Carole what to do to bring her the same pleasure and they made love for hours, made love in all the secretive and delicious ways of lesbians, and then they slept.

Jean awoke in an empty bed, remembering, remembering with no passion to conceal the overwhelming rush of guilt. She was glad that Carole was gone, glad that there was no girl there to accuse her with sullen, hurt eyes.

The worst was yet to come.

And the worst did come. Not that morning, that cold gray morning when Jean stayed home from work in fear and shame.

Later. When she saw the evening paper.

The *Record* carried the story. And it was not a nice story. Not a nice story at all. It was a story about a young girl, a blonde girl, a girl named Carole. Somebody had found her, found her in her own room, at noon, with all her clothing off and her head in the oven.

And the gas on.

Jean never went back to work. There was nothing to connect her with Carole's suicide, nothing to implicate her, nothing to point accusing fingers at her. There was only her own guilt, only the knowledge that, to all intents and purposes, she had murdered Carole as surely as if she had stuck the blonde girl's head in the oven and turned on the gas herself.

She was a murderess. She had seduced a girl, seduced her into something the girl could only conceive of as foul and inhuman perversion, and after the seduction, Carole had found life impossible.

For several weeks Jean had stayed in the apartment, unable to face the world or to face herself. She remained alone, barely eating enough to remain alive, hating herself and her world and the perversion which made her inhuman, a murderess.

At one point she even toyed with the mad notion of going straight, of abandoning her lesbianism and becoming an ordinary woman again, of finding a man, marrying him and settling down. She even went so far as to pick up a man in a bar with the sole purpose of forcing herself to submit to him, to learn to like heterosexual relations, to become a woman instead of a freak.

She couldn't go through with it. The man's touch revolted her. They were in a hotel room he had rented for the express purpose of sleeping with her, and he had her bra off and was squeezing her breasts harshly in his huge hands. She knew what he was going to do and the thought nauseated her. She couldn't submit, couldn't let it happen, not to her, not with him.

She told him to stop, and he wouldn't stop, and finally she had had to stop him. She kicked him square in the groin with all her strength and the man bellowed and pitched forward on his face, holding himself and moaning like a wounded steer.

And she had run away.

She was a lesbian and nothing would change that. So she found a girl again and the game began once more. But she had taken a vow. She would make love only with true lesbians, only with girls who had been there before. She would not seduce anybody. There would never be a another Carole.

And here she was.

•   •   •

Dinner was over. Jean looked around the table, at Terri, and at Joyce. Her hands were trembling slightly and her heart was beating strongly. Too strongly.

She smiled.

So did Terri and Joyce.

"Well," she said, forcing the words out, "where do we go from here?"

CHAPTER 4

Where, Pete Galton wondered, *do we go from here?*

The *we* he used was an editorial we, for Pete Galton was quite alone, seated in the chair in front of the table in his own apartment, looking at but not seeing the wall across the room. His eyes were out of focus and his head was spinning.

Where we do not go, he thought sadly, *is back to the book.* The book, such as it was, had come to a standstill that threatened to be permanent. The book had stopped, quite simply on the very same night that the twin introductions to Sandy and marijuana had been so neatly accomplished. Before he had gone out that night the portable typewriter had been stashed away and the pile of completed manuscript had been placed in a drawer. The manuscript, as far as he knew, still reposed in the drawer. The typewriter, as far as he knew, had neither been lost, strayed, nor stolen. He could not tell for certain, because he had been careful to look at neither manuscript nor typewriter since. He was interested in neither. He did not want to write anything and he did not want to look at what he had written and he especially did not want to think about the whole miserable scene.

He ran his hand over his face, which itched persistently because of his failure to shave. If he went without shaving long enough he would have a beard which would not itch, but for the next couple of weeks he was in a bind. What he had now was not, by any stretch of the imagination, a beard. It was a mess, and it itched, and there was little else to be said about it.

It was Wednesday and since Friday night he had been neatly transplanted to another world, a world that had begun with pot and Sandy. It was a weird world, more bad than good, but a world that he had neither the ability nor the slightest desire to leave for the time being. Just as Sandy had managed to be peculiarly more and less than pure sex, and this at the same time, so the new weird world was more and less than what he wanted. Confusing and weird and difficult to ponder accurately.

So to hell with it.

He had been saying to hell with a great many things lately. It began Saturday morning when he awoke, mouth dry, limbs heavy, but curiously refreshed, more refreshed than he had been in a long time. He had looked around for a trace of Sandy. True to her word, she was gone. No woman slept by his side. But he could still smell the very physical smell of her, could still remember the touch of her. He started to get out of bed, started to dress, and then discovered the brown manila envelope that Sandy had left behind, the marijuana that was her legacy to him.

He remembered that marijuana was illegal, that possession was good for a stretch of a year and a day. His first impulse was to throw it out, flush it down the toilet, or, more sanely, find Sandy again and give it back to her. But something kept him from doing just that. Instead, for some reason which he didn't bother to in-quire into for the moment, he picked up the small envelope and placed it in a drawer in the brown cigarette-scarred dresser.

Then he scrambled four eggs, because he suddenly realized

how very hungry he was, and tossed a chunk of cheddar cheese in with the eggs for flavor. He ate the eggs right out of the aluminum skillet, wolfing them down like a man who had not eaten in days, and was surprised to find that he was still vaguely hungry after he had finished them. He put water on to boil and made himself a cup of instant coffee and toasted bread, which he ate while he waited for the coffee to cool. Then, over coffee, he smoked the first two cigarettes of the morning.

He thought about many things while he smoked the cigarettes and drank the coffee. He thought about the marijuana, about Sandy, about the book, and, inevitably, about Linda. What he did not consider was that his life had changed, that he was not going to work on the book that afternoon, or the next afternoon, or ever, that another plateau on the road to Where-in-hell-are-you-going had come too quickly upon him.

He realized that later, slowly, as he walked through the streets of the Village as he walked every day. It certainly did not come in a flash. It came gradually and in a hundred different tiny ways. It came with sights and sounds, thoughts and unspoken words. It came in a new type of perception of the world around him, a fourteenth way of looking at Wallace Stevens' blackbird, a different manner of hearing sounds and seeing sights and smelling odors.

It was not the marijuana which had done this, nor Sandy, nor anything that simple. It was, in a sense, something that had been building since Linda Medellin had disappeared into thin air, had metamorphosed into somebody else's wife. It had begun, truthfully, perhaps long before that—rooted in the person Peter Galton was and the person he was becoming.

The night, the pot and the woman—catalysts working changes that had to come. Not a new progression but a step along the lines of the old one, a step thoroughly consistent with quitting the job at the *Record* and living behind a typewriter and under a stone.

And so he had walked around, looking at the same people and seeing new faces, walking the same streets on somehow different feet, hearing differently, smelling, tasting and touching differently.

That afternoon he did not wind up back at his apartment settled behind his typewriter. He wound up instead in a tiny jazz club on the Lower East Side with hyper-modern music tearing at his intestines and abstracts on the walls howling at him like geometric banshees. The music had never reached him that way before and the pictures had never made as much sense. Nor did the people in the club—the long-haired girls who looked like Sandy, the hollow-eyed men who looked, to him, now, like himself— ever before seem so thoroughly akin to himself.

He went home alone, wanting to be alone, wasting a dollar on a taxi so that he could get home in a hurry. Then he had paced the floor of his apartment, trying to understand why he had come there, what it was that he had wanted or needed or craved. Then he thought of Sandy, and the envelope, and he knew.

He had never rolled cigarettes before, but he managed to teach himself, remembering the movements that Sandy's fingers had made the night before. The first try didn't work at all and the marijuana spilled on the floor. He had plenty, he could have afforded to leave it there, but something made him pick it all up and return it to the envelope. Then he tried again.

The second attempt was better and the third was better still and as he continued rolling slender cigarettes and twisting their ends, he began to glow with a feeling of accomplishment. He rolled all of the marijuana, making an impressive total of fifteen cigarettes. Ten he returned to the envelope, which he replaced carefully in the dresser drawer. The other five he smoked.

He smoked slowly, alone, the windows of the apartment shut to retain the smoke, his lungs straining to hold in each dragful of smoke as long as he possibly could. He smoked all five of the cigarettes, then fitted the butts, the roaches, into a pipe he had received long ago as a present from Linda. It struck him funny, using the pipe she had given him to smoke marijuana, but he also found something vaguely appropriate in the act.

When he was through smoking, he wanted merely to lie down and think about things. He stretched out on the bed, still fully dressed, and let his mind wander. Hours later the drug began to slip free from his mind. He closed his eyes then and let sleep come to him, deep sleep that was deliciously satisfying.

That had set the pattern. The next day he smoked four more of the marijuana cigarettes immediately after eating breakfast, then went out for a walk as usual. The marijuana was different from liquor and his coordination was unimpaired, his gait steady. The sunlight hurt his eyes and he stopped at the Whelan's at Sixth Avenue and Eighth Street to buy a pair of sunglasses. Then he walked to Washington Square where a crowd of people were gathered around the fountain in the center of the park, playing guitars and banjoes and singing folksongs. He listened to them for a while, then bought a chocolate eclair Good Humor from an Italian vendor and walked over to a bench in the shade to eat it.

He hadn't intended to mention to anybody that he was high on marijuana but he found himself talking about it to the light-skinned Negro girl who sat down beside him. She was a young girl with old eyes and perfect light-coffee skin.

"I could use some, man."

He looked at her and remembered the girl named Sandy. He looked her over carefully, looked at her pointed breasts and her wide hips, and he felt a warm rush of desire.

"I got six joints left," he said, "at my pad."

"Where's your crib at?"

"21 Gay Street."

"Let's go, man."

He remembered Sandy and he decided that it was his marijuana, his apartment, his turn to impose conditions. He knew that she was willing to sleep with him but he decided that he wanted more than that, that there was something special he wanted from her, something on a par with what Sandy had wanted from him.

He told her about it. And she was willing, completely willing, and they left the park with benches and shade trees and folksingers and chess players and walked the several short blocks to Gay Street, number 21, apartment 8-B.

They smoked the six cigarettes before anything else. He was still very high from before and the marijuana he smoked now merely sent him higher and higher, turning him on to brand-new mental and sensual connections, making everything just that much clearer and rosier and greener.

Then they stood up, the two of them, bodies apart, and they began to undress. He watched her remove her clothes and saw that the body beneath them was a good one, a superb one, with firm sloping breasts and strong thighs and wide hips made for love. He looked at her, studied her carefully, and then he sat down on the edge of the bed. Waiting.

She knew her lines. She walked away from him to the opposite side of the room, then turned slowly and headed back toward him. He watched her come, slowly, very slowly, and it was torture to wait for her. But he waited and slowly, very slowly, she came to him.

They were together all that afternoon and all that night. From time to time they slept, and when they awoke their bodies rejoined and locked in combat. She was still there in the morning and he took her fiercely then, awake and hungry. And when it was over he remained in bed while she dressed and left him.

The pattern was set.

Now it was Wednesday and he was alone, smoking ordinary cigarettes with nothing except tobacco in them, wondering where he would go that night, what he would do. He had half-decided to go once again to Ariadne's Web, perhaps to find Sandy, perhaps to meet someone else, perhaps merely to sit and drink red wine.

He thought about the girl who had bothered him on the steps, the girl who smelled of innocence, the girl with sun in her eyes, and he remembered how he had brushed her off, the sound of his own words, the hurt look that momentarily replaced the sun in her eyes. He thought about her and he wondered how she could have looked at him without seeing what he was, that he inhabited a different world and saw different things and lived a different life. He thought about taking the girl to Ariadne's and he had to laugh. She probably would not even know enough to be shocked. She would merely fail to comprehend what was taking place.

He left then, went to Ariadne's, and ran into Sandy. She was glad to see him, or said she was, and there was a party set for that night, and he was invited.

"Too many people," she told him. "Deep people ready to ball. Probably turn into an orgy. They usually turn into orgies. The big sets, I mean, not the small scenes with little people who know each other and like that. The mob scenes where everybody goes to get screaming high and make it with whoever is closest. You probably won't want to come. I wouldn't blame you."

He wanted to come.

"You know Fred Koans?"

He didn't.

"An artist, man. He says so, anyway. Also a poet, also a sculptor, and occasionally a musician. He had real trouble with the last, you dig? I mean, you buy paints, you can fake being a painter. You know what words are, you can fake the poetry scene. You buy clay, you're suddenly a sculptor. But you aren't a musician unless you know how to blow an instrument. He got lucky."

"How?"

"Bongo drums. You buy bongo drums, you're a musician. It's a cruel world. Art doesn't support Freddie. So he has parties. His friends come free. The Madison Avenue types who want to learn what hip is pay ten bucks apiece. He thinks he's conning them. They think they're conning him. It's a funny world."

"Where do I fit?"

"You'd come with me," she said, "but somebody else already picked up the option. You want to go and you don't know Freddie, it's ten dollars. Can you make it?"

"I suppose so."

"There's pot and juice and more women than you can shake a stick at. If you feel like coming on, it's at 347 Saint Marks Place. East Side. You know it?"

He nodded.

"Fall by, baby. I like you, I think. Fall by and I'll save some of it for you. Won't that be nice?"

He agreed that it would be nice. He got up and left, wondering why he should bother wasting ten dollars on a party that would probably be filled to overflowing with advertising men. Then he decided that, actually, he really did want to go. He didn't know why.

It was silly. If he wanted a woman he could find a woman without looking very far. Women were easy to find when you had the key. When you knew where to look and what to look for, women were very easy to find.

And getting high wasn't what was drawing him there. He had been high before. He could get high again. He could do this for considerably less than ten dollars.

Why, then?

Why run all the way over to Saint Marks Place, paying ten dollars for the privilege of enjoying the company of a batch of people whom he would not like in the least.

Why?

He figured out the answer. The answer was embodied in one word she had said, one single word in a long stream of words. *Orgy.* She had said the party would be an orgy and he had never been to an orgy and it suddenly seemed very important to him to go to an orgy. He did not know why. Unless, perhaps, it was because he would be plumbing the depths of a new desperation, sinking into the middle of a new sort of sickness.

Again, why?

But that was hard to answer, impossible to answer, unpleasant to even think about. He decided not to think about it and followed his feet back to 21 Gay Street, to his apartment, so that he could pick up a ten-dollar bill and buy his way into an orgy.

Joyce Kendall didn't quite know what to make of it. The two girls, Jean and Terri, were very friendly. The conversation was as pleasant as the meal had been delicious. She talked about Schwerners-ville and about Clifton and about her job. They talked about New York and about their own work.

She began to get the feeling that something was going on which she didn't understand. The looks exchanged between the two of them—nothing she could pin down, but something from which she felt somehow excluded. The way one or the other of them would say something which would seem to have two meanings, the one she understood and the one shared by the two girls.

It was disconcerting.

Oh, nonsense. She decided that she was making a big production out of nothing. Of course she was left out of part of the mood. After all, they had known each other for ages and here she was meeting them for the first time. You could hardly expect a relationship to blossom in which she instantly was party to all their backlog of experience. That was ridiculous.

Still, the looks and the double meanings and—

Terri stood up. "I have to run," she announced. "There's an artist waiting to paint me. He's lousy but he's also loaded. One of those jokers who paints creamy nudes for the creeps to buy in the outdoor art show. Terrible stuff, painted by a terrible guy and sold to terrible people. But it's money and I have to go earn some. I'll see you, people. Nice meeting you, Joyce. Be good. Don't do anything I wouldn't do."

"That gives her a lot of leeway," Jean said.

They laughed.

But, Joyce thought, again there seemed to be a hidden meaning in the conversation. She couldn't pin it down, of course, but an ordinary parting rejoinder had suddenly taken on the garb of something more than that.

"Joyce? Come on in and have a seat. I'll put a stack of records on the player."

She sat on the couch and Jean sat in the chair. There was an expression on Jean's face now that was a new one, an unfamiliar one. Again—and it was becoming standard procedure now—it was one she couldn't pin down, couldn't define, couldn't place, couldn't categorize.

They sat in silence. The music was unfamiliar, too-modern

classical music, harsh, strident, discordant. She did not like it at all.

Then Jean smiled.

Here we go, Jean was thinking. *Here we go. The windup, the pitch, and out of the park.*

It would have been better if Joyce was either unattractive or obviously gay. One way or the other the fencing would be done with, the games would be dispensed with, the party would be either on or off and no two ways about it.

But now—

Now she was sitting in her apartment with a beautiful girl who was not, unfortunately, a lesbian. Which gave her two alternatives. She could forget sexual interest in the girl, or she could come right out and tell the girl what was coming off. Either way would be, at least, honorable. Either way she would be avoiding the type of mess that had happened with Carole. Either way, win or lose, she would be able to look at herself in the mirror.

The sensible thing, of course, would be to forget the girl, to let her be a friend but to keep sex out of the picture. The sensible thing, she knew, was not going to work in this particular instance. Joyce Kendall was just too goddamned attractive. Any girl with a face like hers and hair like hers and breasts like hers and a behind like hers was just . . . too . . . God!

Jean sighed. She wanted to come right and tell the girl, to blurt out *I'm a lesbian and I want to lay you*. But she couldn't bring herself to do it. She liked Joyce, liked her as well as desired her, and she didn't want to hurt or shock the girl. She wanted to lead up to it slowly.

"Joyce," she said, "do you have much to do with men?"

The girl's eyebrows went up.

"I used to."

"But not now?"

"I don't know anybody."

Jean nodded. "I don't mean to pry," she said. "But did you ever . . . do anything with a man? You know what I mean."

The girl colored.

"That is—"

"I'm not a virgin."

"More than one man?"

"Two."

"Recently?"

"Not for over a year."

The answer made her hopeful. If Joyce had been sleeping around and then had stopped, there was probably a reason for it. And the probable reason was that she hadn't been satisfied. Something must have been missing. The girl was probably a lesbian, a lesbian who didn't yet know the truth about herself. Jean's mouth went dry with anticipation. She would be the one to teach the girl everything, to show her the meaning of love, real love, not the sort of mess that men and women went through but the true and beautiful love that only two women could share.

It would be the first time for Joyce. She would be a willing pupil and Jean would be a more than willing teacher.

"Did you enjoy it?"

Joyce was puzzled. "Of course I enjoyed it," she said. "Why wouldn't I enjoy it?"

"Some women don't, you know."

"You mean frigid women?"

"No," Jean said slowly, carefully. "Some women just don't enjoy sex with a man."

"I do."

"Are you sure?"

"Of course I'm sure. What kind of a question is that? What do you mean?"

"Maybe I can explain."

Her hands trembling, Jean got up from the chair and sat on the couch next to Joyce. She couldn't stop staring at the girl. She looked at her breasts, imagining what they would feel like, smell like, taste like—what it would be like to stroke them and cup them and play with them.

Mentally, she pictured Joyce welcoming her advances, submitting to them, glorying in the parade of brand-new sensations. She imagined the way Joyce would moan softly when Jean's lips closed over a nipple, playing with it, tugging at it, until the long-haired girl would go out of her mind, with passions that were new to her.

"Joyce," she said softly, "some women don't enjoy sex with men. Or they think they do, but that's because they don't know what they are missing. There's a lot that women like that are missing. Do you understand?"

"Frankly, I don't. And—"

It was hard now, very hard. And she knew that she was going to lose, for the moment at least, that she was going to shock and stun the girl no matter how hard she tried to be gentle and slow with her. Joyce would leave and Jean would not have the sweetness of the girl beneath her, the bulging breasts swelling in her hands.

But she could not stop.

"Joyce," she said, "Terri and I . . . we're different."

Joyce's eyes went very wide. They held a vague, faint glimmering of recognition.

"We . . . we are . . ."

"Go ahead."

"Terri and I are lesbians."

That did it, Jean thought. That shot the works. The horror and nausea in the girl's eyes was unmistakable. There was no way to rationalize it. She was not only uninterested. She was literally sick.

"You . . . sleep with each other?"

"That's right."

"You like it that way?"

"That's right, Joyce. But—"

"And you want me to be like you? You want me to be a lesbian and sleep with you?"

"Joyce—"

The girl was standing now, her hands outstretched to defend herself, to keep this evilness away from her.

"I thought you liked me," she was saying. "I thought you wanted me to be your friend. I was just trying to be friendly. I just wanted to have somebody to talk to. And all the time you were thinking about what I'd be like in bed. All the time you wanted to get my clothes off and . . . and—"

"Joyce—"

"Stay away from me! Damn you, stay away from me! I'm not a

lesbian. And I don't want to see what it's like or to see you or your girl friend or to talk to you or to have anything to do with you or to, or, oh, oh leave me alone!"

Then she was running for the door, tears streaking her pretty face. Jean made no move to stop her, called no words after her, stayed instead where she was and thought about what had happened. What had happened was not good. What had happened was horrible, as a matter of fact.

She had been so sure about the girl for a moment there. But it had all backfired, had all blown up in her face. Now she was alone, frustrated, unable to sit still and unable to cease hating herself.

She cried, finally. But even that didn't seem to do the least bit of good.

Joyce locked the door of her apartment, ran to the bedroom and threw herself down on the bed. She had never felt quite so horrible in her life. Even the first shock of the break-up with Joe Cardigan had been nothing compared with this.

It was terrible.

She had never met a lesbian before, had never even thought much about homosexuality. She had read a book once, a book by an author named Lesley Evans, a book entitled *Strange Are The Ways of Love*. The book had been about lesbians and she thought back to the girls in the book and wondered if she could be like them. No, she decided, she couldn't.

Then why had Jean wanted to—?

She didn't understand. All she knew, all she could think of, was that her loneliness before was nothing compared to the loneliness she felt now. Now she was lonely, now she was alone in a very private portion of a very private Hell.

Jean and Terri had been the only friendly people she had met. The only ones. And why were they friendly? Because they were after her. Because they were interested in taking her to bed. That was all they wanted. Joyce Kendall as a person didn't mean a damned thing to them. Joyce Kendall was only important as somebody to seduce, somebody to kiss and touch and take to bed.

God!

That was all anybody wanted, she thought. People were only interested in themselves, in what they could get. People were mean and rotten and narrow and self-seeking. She would do better keeping to herself in her apartment, working at her job, living her own life.

But the loneliness . . .

The loneliness that covered everything like a shroud. The loneliness that, even now, while she was still reeling with the shock and horror of discovery, made her think for a fleeting moment that maybe it wouldn't be so bad to sleep with Jean, to live with the two of them, because that way at least somebody would talk to her, somebody would pay attention to her, somebody would like her and spend time with her and care about her.

God!

She had to find somebody. She had to find somebody or go mad trying. Somebody somewhere would want her. If it was a man, and all the man wanted was to sleep with her, well, even that was better than nothing. She would sleep with a man if she had to. Just so she wouldn't be so completely alone.

The apartment was a trap. She got up from the bed and went to the door. She went outside and started off down the block, not very much caring where she was going, who she would meet, what they would do. She knew only that, whoever he was, she had to find him.

The rest didn't matter.

She walked quickly, and then, suddenly, she saw him and raced into his arms.

To say that Pete Galton was surprised when Joyce Kendall threw herself into his arms is to make what might well be the understatement of the century. He was overwhelmed. For a minute he couldn't remember who in hell she was. Then he remembered. Of course. The cornfed thing who wanted somebody to talk to. Hell of a way for an innocent cornfed thing to act.

"Listen to me," she was saying. "Just listen to me. I know you don't like me and I don't care. I just want to be with you or I'll go out of my mind. I need somebody. I'm alone all the time and I can't stand it. I don't care who you are or what you want or where you take me. I just can't stand it if I'm alone all by myself for another minute."

It was so funny he wanted to laugh.

"Please," she said.

He thought for a few seconds. Then he smiled slowly, remembering where he was going, to the apartment of the artist-of-sorts named Fred Koans.

He wondered what it would be like to see Little Miss Cornball at a first-class orgy.

He decided it might be interesting. Very interesting. It would cost twenty bucks instead of ten, but it just might be worth it.

"Relax," he told her, stroking her soft hair. "You just relax, baby. You can come with me."

"You mean it?"

"Sure," he said. "We'll have a ball, baby. We're going to a party."

"I—"

"You wait right here," he said. "I got to get some money. I'll be right back."

"Wait," she said. "I'll come with you. I don't want to be alone."

He looked at her—at her hair, her face, her breasts, her hips.

"Sure," he said. "Come on."

CHAPTER 5

They walked east. Night was filtering down on New York, making its way slowly through the dense and smoky air. The sky darkened. While most New Yorkers lived their entire lives without so much as catching a glimpse of the sky, all New Yorkers knew that the sky was there, and believed in it with the same blind faith with which a man believes there is a God in heaven and gold in Fort Knox.

Periodically, New Yorkers receive evidence of the existence of a sky. When it rains, the rain has obviously come from some place. The sun, which occasionally lights up New York for brief periods of time, also has to come from some place. This mythical place, understood but rarely seen, is called sky.

Now the sky grew dark. The streets were still warm, with the buildings holding in the heat and preventing it from rising. Washington Square was cooler but when they had crossed the park and continued east on Fourth Street, the heat came back again.

She talked and he half-listened. She didn't really care whether he was listening or not—he was there, and little else mattered to her for the moment. He was there—someone, someone to listen, someone to be with, someone to ease the impossible loneliness. Now he was taking her somewhere—God knew where—and she was going, and she did not know what was going to happen. But she knew that she was not going to be alone, not for a little while anyway, and that was enough for the time being.

He was a good-looking man, she noticed, ruggedly attractive and, well, sexy-looking. She liked the look of his hands and his arms and his face, and she was ashamed to find herself wondering what he would look like if he took his clothing off. The thoughts embarrassed and excited her. She pictured him naked, towering over her, reaching for her with hungry eyes.

The palms of her hands beaded with sweat. *God*, she thought, *I need it more than I thought. I need it from a man, soon. A man who will do it to me and make everything good again. A man like this one. A man with strength and hunger and passion.*

The thoughts shamed her, but they also excited her again, and she wondered if perhaps she was abnormal, a freak, a girl who was ready to stretch out on her back the minute a man was sufficiently aware of her to acknowledge her existence.

Maybe she would sleep with him and maybe she wouldn't. First they were going to a party, and then, if he was nice to her at the party and if she had a good time, then she would let him come inside her apartment for a while. And then hands would grip her breasts and hands would run up under her skirt and touch her and hands would strip her of her clothing and ease her back down onto her bed.

She shivered, then thought again of the impending party, forcing her thoughts away from sex and lust and passion. It would be nice, she decided. It had been a long time since she had gone to a party. She hardly remembered what parties were like.

Maybe, she thought, she would meet some nice people. Maybe once you met people socially, you didn't keep getting left out of things. A pleasant party, some nice people—then she would be set on her feet again, alive again.

She hoped it would be a nice party.

Saint Marks Place was a small street, narrow, relatively pleasant. There was a jazz club on one block, a few art galleries on another block, a church here and there, a political clubroom. He found the address without any trouble and led her inside and up two flights of stairs. He didn't need to look at the mailboxes or doorbells to figure out which apartment belonged to Fred Koans. All he had to do was follow his ears.

A tall, thin, very dark Negro stood at the door. He looked at the two of them very deliberately, as if trying to determine whether or not they were ones who should pay. Pete caught on at once, left his money in his wallet, and spoke in a low voice, gravelly and soft.

"Sandy make it yet?"

"All girls are named Sandy," the Negro said. "It's the most recent development since Shirley. Did you have any particular Sandy in mind?"

"Long hair."

"All Sandys have long hair. It's inevitable."

"Sandy from Ariadne's," Pete said. "Sandy from the Fishhook."

"Oh," the Negro said. "*That* Sandy. Crazy. Come on in."

"In" was a huge single room, a loft converted into something approaching living quarters. It seemed, however, as though no one lived there. There was only the one room plus a bathroom and that left no place for Fred Koans to sleep, unless he curled up on the cushions that were scattered around the floor. Another possibility occurred to Pete. Maybe the guy was really a professional. Maybe he rented the loft solely for parties and had the intelligence to live somewhere else.

There were perhaps fifty people in the huge room, about a third of them looking like the Sunday supplement stereotype of the beatnik, another third looking as though they had been born in their gray flannel suits. The remaining third just looked like people. Ordinary people.

It wasn't hard to spot Fred Koans. The man was huge, to begin with. He would have showed up anyplace. He was well over six-four, with a massive barrel chest and forearms like legs of mutton. A huge red beard hung like an oriole's nest from his face and his moustache curled upward in the handlebar style. His hair was red-brown, a shade darker than the beard, and he had a high fore-head.

Of course, since Pete had never received so much as a descrip-tion of Koans, the man's appearance was not enough for identi-fication. But there were other subtle clues. There was the large congo drum which he gripped between his knees and pounded in a monotonous but stubbornly catchy rhythm. And, more im-portant, there was the extreme air of command. He, obviously, was the man in charge. You could tell that both by the way he surveyed the room and by the way everyone looked at him.

Pete glanced around again, then remembered suddenly that he was not there alone, that he had brought a girl with him. He was sorry now that he had bothered to bring her. He had noticed a lot of females whom he wouldn't mind making, and now this chick was along, and he was stuck with her.

In which case, the obvious thing to do was to unload her.

"Joyce—"

She looked at him. Her eyes were wide and it wasn't too difficult to see that she was greatly impressed by the party. Which was natural enough. The expression on her face, however, indicated that she was enchanted rather than alarmed.

That would change.

"Cut loose," he ordered. "Mingle. Walk around. Talk to people. It's the only way."

She seemed puzzled.

"At these parties," he improvised, "it's best not to stay in one place too long. Move around. Get acquainted. Otherwise it looks as though we're uptown squares or something."

Which was a strange sort of logic but which evidently made its own kind of sense to her. She nodded dumbly and began to walk away in no particular direction.

He immediately chose the opposite direction and began to see what was happening.

Plenty was.

He ran into Sandy, to start things rolling. She was standing in a corner with a thin young man who looked at the world through nearly opaque glasses. He had a bad case of acne.

The girl seemed very willing to turn her attentions from Pimple Puss to Pete. She smiled, a big hello smile, and said she was glad to see he had made it.

"You were putting me on," he said.

"Huh?"

"The ten buck bit."

"You didn't have to pay?"

"Nope," he said. "Brought a chick and she didn't have to pay either. But I'll forgive you."

"I wasn't putting you on," she said. "Never figured you'd make it on a freebie bit. Who was on the door?"

He described the Negro.

"You must look sick," she said. "Aces only lets sick cats in for nothing. I guess you're sick."

"I guess so."

"Kiss me, sick man."

The Pimply One had happily disappeared. Pete took Sandy in his arms, brought her up close and pressed his mouth to hers. Her tongue was a serpent snaking into his mouth and her arms came around him and held him close. He could feel the burning warmth of her breasts through the thin material of his shirt.

He kissed her again. Then she stepped back, took his hand and pressed it tight against her breast for a few seconds. She dropped it and grinned.

"Later," she said. "Plenty of time later."

"Now what happens?"

"A party."

"Pot?"

She shook her head. "Not a chance," she said. "Too many people. Freddie usually gets a turnout of twenty tops. He's got fifty now. Fifty people try to make a pot scene and the fuzz descends like a ton of crud."

"Then what?"

She smiled. "You have a drink yet?"

"No."

"Have one."

"Something in the drinks?"

She grinned. "Like you could put it that way. It's this new

drug, like it's even legal if you have a prescription. Freddie conned this doctor type into writing for him."

"What does the drug do?"

"Like pot," she said. "Change your perception of reality. But with a difference."

"What's the difference?"

She grinned wider than before. "Like a sex stimulant," she said. "A dose of this and you start to itch and burn a little. And pretty soon everybody's on the floor with everybody else. It makes quite a party."

He could understand that.

She patted his arm. "You got to give me one more squeeze," she said, "and then you got to go pick up on a drink. This stuff works fast. Pretty soon things get moving. You don't want to be left out of it, do you?"

"I guess not."

"So squeeze me. Ooooooh, that's right. Now give a squeeze as hard as you possibly can. Ooooooh! Too much, baby! You go get that drink now before I don't let you go. Hurry!"

He forced himself to walk away from her and found a long wooden table with paper cups full of liquid set out on it. He took one of the cups and drained it in a single swallow. The cup contained mainly grape juice. He couldn't even taste the added ingredient.

For the hell of it he had another cup.

He didn't feel any differently but he knew that he would in a moment or two. He walked away from the table, looking for a big-breasted girl to roll around on the floor with.

•   •   •

The Professor was holding court. He was a stringy man with long arms and long legs and a long face, not a real professor at all. As a matter of fact, he made his living as a shoplifter. He was not a snatch-and-grab artist at all, but a very careful and very selective shoplifter. He stole only what he either wanted for himself or knew that he could fence for a good price.

He patronized book stores, department stores, jewelry stores, pawn shops and small neighborhood stores. He worked a wide territory. He made enough money to live comfortably, worked his own hours, and enjoyed his work greatly.

The two men he was talking to, boys really, were apprentices of his. He was working both ends with them, setting up their scores, buying their loot from them and reselling it to his own fence at a profit. The two young men had nothing but respect for the Professor. He was a professional and they were just getting out of the amateur class. They thought he was great.

"You see that girl?"

They saw her.

"The first thing one would notice," said the Professor, "is the great physical appeal of the girl. You probably have noticed breasts and hips first of all. I trust they have passed inspection. I, on the other hand, have been noticing the face. The face is the most important part. Character and experience show up in the face. She has a good face."

The two men nodded. As the Professor had guessed, they were now noticing Joyce Kendall's face for the first time. But the breasts and hips had already made a tremendous impression upon both of them.

"If you look at the face," the Professor continued, "and if you are an astute observer of such things, you can discover a good many things about the girl. Insights into her personality, her background, her moral character."

"Like if she's good in the sack?"

"Don't be coarse," the Professor said. "Essentially, that is what I was referring to. There are other things to be learned as well. Would you care to hear me enumerate them?"

"Sure," they chorused.

"To begin," the Professor said, "the girl is not a native of this city. She is from another part of the country, probably the Midwest. She has been in New York a short period of time. Less than a month, I would guess."

The two boys nodded.

"In addition," said the Professor, "she has no idea of the true purpose of this party. She is wandering around lost, digging everything because it's real, as it were. If she had any idea that she is going to conclude this evening in an incredibly physical manner, she would be greatly surprised, if not horrified."

"Would she like it, Professor?"

The Professor sighed. "She has not had much experience but she is a passionate girl. She shall enjoy it. She shall feel uncomfortable about it in the future, but she shall enjoy it."

"All this you can tell from her face?"

"All this," the Professor assured them. "Now I have a suggestion to make to the two of you. You may be interested and you may not. Would you like to hear what it is?"

"Sure."

"Fill us in, Professor."

"Hit us with it."

The Professor sighed wearily. "As you may have guessed," he said, "I find this girl intriguing. I think of her as something special. She excites me."

They nodded.

"I think we should make love to her."

"*We?*"

"Like all of us?"

"Of course," said the Professor. "In turn. Each, needless to say, in a different manner. For the sake of variety. We wouldn't want to bore the poor girl."

One of the apprentices made an obvious comment.

The Professor sighed again. Why was it, he wondered, that he was doomed to have dolts for associates? The answer, he decided quickly, was simple. Dolts were easier to exploit.

"I shall approach her," he went on. "I've watched her take one drink so far. Soon she shall have had five more drinks. That makes a total of six," he added. He always liked to spell things out for his associates. Even arithmetic gave them a hard time on occasion.

"Six?"

"Six."

"That's one hell of a lot, Professor. A girl has six of those and she's out on her ear. I mean, you could put it like the sex urge is all she's got left. Like she turns into a sex machine."

"I know."

"But—"

"My boy," said the Professor fondly, "if you would listen for just a moment, I will fill your ears with a dose of eternal wisdom that will ease your lot in life immeasurably."

The boy looked blank. "So?"

"Just this," said the Professor. "If you keep your mouth shut at all times you will find it considerably more difficult to plant your foot in it."

The Professor smiled briefly, an engaging smile, and walked over to Joyce Kendall.

Boom-ba-da-da-da-boom. Boo-boppa-boom-boom-boom. Boo-boppa-boom-boom-boom.

Fred Koans gripped the congo drum tight between his knees and pounded it furiously. He dug himself on drums. He liked the punishing feel of the taut leather under his hands, the way his fingers stung pleasurably from the blows, the resonance of the drum, the pulsing monotony of the beat.

Boom-ba-da-da-boom. Bo-boppa-boom-boom-boom. Boo-boppa-boom-boom-boom.

He looked around the large loft and was happy. The stuff in the grape juice was a good idea—better than pot, legal, cheap. A good idea.

And taking effect.

Bo-ba-da-da-boom.

In one corner, a man and a woman had already gotten started. They were well on their way. Both were still fully dressed, but the man's hand was already under the girl's skirt and the girl was obviously enjoying what he was doing.

Boo-boppa-boom-boom-boom-boom.

Two other girls had already removed their sweaters. They were not with men yet but they were attracting attention. One of them had large breasts. The breasts were not perfectly shaped but the quantity compensated for the slight lack of quality. The girl was walking around looking like a free and unfettered spirit.

Boom-boom-boom. Ba-ba-ba-boom-boom. Boom. Boom. Ba-da-da-da-da-da-da-da-doom.

Fred Koans was happy. To begin with, there was better than two hundred bucks in the till. The loft rented for forty a month. Twenty for refreshments and twenty more to the cop on the beat. That left a hundred and a half, maybe a little more, for the private use of one Fred Koans.

Which was very nice.

Boom-ba-boom-boom.

Nice indeed.

Boom-boom-boom.

It was his biggest party so far, the most nicely attended, and Fred Koans loved to throw parties. Before he had devised the miraculous gambit of throwing beat parties for squares to buy their way into, he had thrown beat parties that didn't net him a cent. Hell, they cost him money.

But it was worth it.

Boom-ba-boom.

Well worth it.

Ba-boom.

It was worth it because Freddie was the perfect host. A good host is a person who enjoys being a host, not somebody who gives a party just to pay back previous hosts. A good host enjoys watching people drink his liquor and have a good time.

There was never a better host than Freddie. He stationed

himself at the bongo drums at the beginning of the evening and didn't get up until the end of the evening if he could help it. He stayed where he was, drumming away and watching his friends have a good time. That was what he liked best.

Boom-da-boom.

Other cats threw parties. But they weren't like Freddie. Other cats would try to pick up on chicks themselves, to cut out some of the guests.

Not Freddie.

He stayed at the drum, beat the drum, watched the people, watched them having a good time.

Boom-boom-boom.

Watched them drink, smoke, talk.

Boom-boom.

Watched them take off their clothing and kiss each other and stroke each other and rub up against each other. Watched them neck and pet and feel and kiss. Watched them get down on the floor on a cushion or not on a cushion. Watched them make love.

Because, you see, that was Freddie's kick. He liked to watch people. It was much more fun for him than *doing* anything, you see.

BOOM!

CHAPTER 6

Terri was tired and her feet hurt. The pose that joker of an artist had made her hold was a lulu—up on her toes, nude, arms stretched forward, knees bent slightly, breasts thrusting out. The breasts thrust out automatically but the rest of the pose was a pain in the neck.

She hesitated outside the door of 21 Gay Street. Jean was inside, her Jean—and, probably, that little bitch Joyce was in there too. It had been hell to go away and leave the two of them alone. But she knew better than to try reforming Jean. Jean was a passionate girl. When she saw a woman who appealed to her, Terri's presence, mental or physical, wasn't enough to restrain her from cruising like a maniac.

Terri knew what to do. You let Jean have her little fling, her hot-pillow games and tongue-darting ecstasy, and then you waited for her to tire of the new one and come back home to Terri where she belonged. Sometimes it took a few days, but inevitably the crush wore off and Terri and Jean were together again. The sort of girl who got jealous easily and let her jealousy show would never be able to hold Jean long. But Terri could. They had been together a long time already. They might well remain together forever, as they fervently assured each other they would in moments of passion.

Terri's finger hesitated in front of the bell. Suppose they were at it right now? It seemed unlikely—Joyce certainly came on straight enough. But you could never tell, and it wouldn't do to interrupt Jean at a time like that.

She gave the bell a very brief jab and waited. The answering buzz came and she pushed open the door and rushed up the flight of stairs, happy now, happy that Jean was alone and waiting for her, happy that Joyce had been either straight or unattracted by Jean, happy that she and Jean would be together now.

"Darling! I missed you. Come inside. I'll build you a drink, honey."

She followed the short-haired woman into the apartment, thinking that Jean was always sweet and solicitous when she was feeling guilty over a successful or attempted infidelity. They clinked glasses and drank.

"Hard day, honey?"

"Terrible. The bastard made me hold a pose forever and I can't stand on my feet any more."

"Poor baby. Sit down then."

Terri sat down. "That's not all," she went on. "The bastard also made his first and last pass at me."

"Why, that—"

"Oh, it's nothing. They all do at one time or another, unless they're fags. I expect it by now. I was wondering what was taking him so long."

"What did you do?"

"I told him I wasn't interested."

"Did you say why?"

"Uh-huh. I told him I was gay. And at first he didn't believe me. He laughed. Then I finally convinced him that I wasn't kidding around, and he developed a brand-new theory of his own."

"What was it?"

Terri grinned. "He said I should let him make love to me, even if I didn't want to, because he was so good at it that I would see the difference between a man and a woman and straighten out. I think he thought it was a new approach."

"What did you tell him? I hope you kicked his face in. What did you say?"

"I told him I was willing."

"What!"

"Hold on. I told him there were just two conditions. I would let him make love to me but first he had to do two things. He had to grow breasts and he had to geld himself. That sort of killed his interest in the whole deal."

They laughed.

"How about you?" Terri's eyes were serious now. "What happened with the little girl from Iowa?"

"I'm sorry, Terri."

"Sorry because you did or sorry because you didn't?"

"Sorry because I wanted to."

Terri reached for a cigarette. She put it between her lips and accepted a light from Jean. She drew the smoke deep into her lungs and held it for a long time. Then she expelled the smoke in a single thin column that held together until it reached the ceiling. Then it broke up, crawled along the ceiling and disappeared.

"It's all right, Jean," she said.

"But it isn't."

"I love you, Jean. And I understand you. You see a girl and

you get excited and you have to do what you have to do. I'm not a jealous bitch. I know you come back to me."

"Always. Forever."

"So I can accept this. Do you want to talk about it?"

"Won't it bother you?"

Terri shook her head.

"I wanted her," Jean said. "You could tell that. I guess I made it pretty obvious."

"Kind of. Go on."

"She's straight. Completely straight. So straight it took me ten minutes of careful explicit conversation before I could get her to the point where she realized I was a lesbian."

"And then?"

"And then she hit three ceilings, cracked completely, and got the merry Hell out of here as if the whole Prussian army was chasing her. I never saw anybody panic so completely."

"Must have been rough."

"For her and for me, too. She was shook, of course. She kept saying how terrible it was. Not because of what I wanted to do, but because that was the only reason I talked to her. You must have seen how lonely she was. Ready to crawl the walls. I thought it was sex—that she wanted somebody to take care of her, whether she knew it or not. But that's not it, or if it is, it's only a small part of it. She's terribly lonely. And now she thinks the only way to get a friend is to put out."

"Poor kid."

"Poor Jean, too. I was crawling the walls. Honest to God, I was ready to scream. I never touched her, Terri, but I thought about it. It was all I could think of. And the more I thought about it the worse it got, and when she left it didn't get any better. You know me, honey. I've got a short fuse."

"And the fuse burned up?"

"The fuse burned up and the powder hasn't gone off yet. I . . . I've had a rough time. A very rough time."

"Poor baby."

"And I kept thinking about Carole—you remember, I told you about Carole, the one who killed herself—I kept thinking about Carole, and I thought what a rotten bitch I was, and at the same time I thought how much I needed it, really ached all over for it, and—"

"I know, honey."

"It was pretty horrible."

"It must have been."

"And that poor kid."

Terri finished her cigarette, stubbed it out in an ashtray on the coffee table. She looked at Jean, her eyes soft now, warm with love and compassion.

"Do you feel better now?"

"Well, I—"

"Of course you don't. You're all wound up, aren't you? Poor honey. You were all ready for love and then you got let down hard. I know how you feel."

"I'm all right, Terri."

"But you want me, don't you? You want me to make everything all right again, don't you?"

"Terri—"

"Let's make love, Jean."

"I don't want to take advantage of you. It's not fair to you,

Terri. To use you when I'm all hot over another woman. It's a bitchy trick, Terri. I won't do it."

"Of course you will."

"Terri—"

"Listen to me, Jean. Listen to me for a minute. I love you, do you hear? And you love me. You play around but you love me and that's all that should ever matter to either of us. See? And I want you. Right now I want you. I want us both to get undressed and slip into bed and I want it to be very slow and very gentle. Do you see what mean?"

"But—"

"No buts. If you're hot over her it'll change in a few seconds. Then you'll be hot over me, because I'm going to give you something to get hot over. Now you stand up from that chair and take off your clothing. Every last stitch of it. And then get under the covers and wait for me."

"Terri, I—"

"You do what I say, Jean. I'm not kidding. You do what I say or I'll rape you!"

It was slow and it was gentle and it was very very good. For a long while before they lay inches apart in the bed, relaxing. Waiting, preparing. They talked in whispers and the words they spoke were love words.

It began slowly and it continued slowly and then it began to grow, building up steam, racing, charging. For Terri it meant that everything was all right again, that Jean was hers, hers alone now and forever, that they were in love and that very little else in the world mattered at all.

For Jean it was that and more, a necessary release, a release she would have gone through hell without.

When it was over, when they recovered their breath again, Terri took Jean's head in her hands and placed Jean's face between her own warm breasts. She felt the softness of Jean's cheek against the inside of each breast. It was warm and clean and good.

They slept like that.

Meanwhile, back at the orgy, things were beginning to move.

In all directions.

Pete Galton was having one hell of a time. With two glasses of Elixer of Votz percolating happily in his bloodstream, Pete was in the mood for love. And, with many many girls suddenly finding it a very hip thing to remove their sweaters, Pete was yet more in the mood for love. He bumbled around, looking for a woman, and deciding that he could afford to be choosy. With all this flesh at his disposal, he didn't have to take the first that came his way.

A girl approached him, wearing the uniform of nudity from the waist up. She had purple eye-shadow sort of gumming up her eyes, but outside of that her face wasn't too bad. Young, sickeningly young, but not bad.

"Hey, baby," she cooed raspingly. "Wanta have a ball?"

He looked at her breasts. They were small and, young as the chick was, they already had a little sag to them. He had the feeling that if she were to lie down on her back, the breasts would disappear entirely, becoming indistinguishable from the rest of the surplus flesh on her stocky frame.

"Well? Wanna have a ball?"

He reached out a hand. He cupped a breast and squeezed it. It was very soft and, evidently, very sensitive as well. She gurgled in joy and closed her eyes in what was probably passion.

"Come on," she said. "I can't wait. Right away, here and now, come on, strip me, come on, hurry up. Please. Right now, take me, now."

Hell, he thought. There had to be something better around than this one.

So he let go of her breast and pulled away from her. "Go find somebody else," he told her.

"What?"

"Somebody else," he said. "Find somebody else and fall on the floor with him."

She looked at him. She took his hand and placed it on her breast.

"Squeeze," she commanded.

He squeezed.

She gasped. "God," she said. "That does nothing to you? Nothing at all?" Her eyes were begging him but they just weren't reaching him at all.

"Sure," he said agreeably. "It does something to me."

"What does it do?"

"It makes me want to find another girl," he said reasonably, withdrawing his hand and pulling away.

She called him the foulest name she could think of and spat at his back. And missed.

●　　●　　●

The Professor was about to capture the rewards of diligent preparation and careful work. With incalculable skill he had managed to get five more glasses of drugged grape juice down the pretty throat of Joyce Kendall. He had watched in amusement as the drug had begun to go to work. Her eyes grew glazed and she stared blankly ahead. That was the beginning. Then he watched as she began to squirm uncomfortably while she talked to him, her neat behind making delicious little maneuvers.

He decided that she was ready.

The next problem, of course, was one of cutting her off from the pack. The sexual pleasure of the girl was one thing, but it was certainly not all there was to it. If that had been the case, the Professor would not have bothered with the notion of letting his two apprentices have a crack at her. He would have saved her for himself, to have and to hold, until he was bored with her.

No, there was more to it than that. The girl might be other than a virgin but she was definitely not the type for an orgy. Therefore, the best use to put her to, in addition to the usual, was humiliating her. The Professor knew Mankind and knew himself. He knew that, from time to time, he could take great pleasure in another's discomfort. Not physical pain—that kind of sadism struck the Professor as meaningless, crude, barbaric, and not sufficiently painful. Degradation and self-loathing hurt worse than the rack or the lash or the iron maiden.

Thus, if he removed the girl from the orgy atmosphere and put her through her own private orgy, it would all be that much worse to her. She would think that she and she alone was sick, that she had submitted to several men while everybody else had a civilized party. She would find out the truth in time, but it would give her a few bad moments, and that was roses with the Professor.

Which was why, as soon as he got the final glass of wine into her, he steered Joyce Kendall into the bathroom and locked the door.

Joyce didn't know why she was in the bathroom. Nor could she figure out what the Professor was doing in the room with her. It was too much to think about.

And she didn't have much chance to think because the Professor was kissing her.

He had one arm around her, holding her close, and he had his mouth glued to hers and his tongue deep inside her mouth, and his free hand was touching her, caressing her, teasing her.

And suddenly Joyce knew, knew more clearly than she had known anything before in her life, just what it was that she wanted.

She wanted a man.

Any man.

And there was a man with her. The professor. Kissing her, holding her, touching her.

His hands tore her clothing off, pushed her to the floor. The bathroom had once had a tile floor; now most of the tiles were cracked or missing. The broken tiles scratched her but somehow she did not notice.

She noticed the man, his hands poking at her breasts, his breath in her face, his body upon her body. She dug her nails into his back and sank her teeth into his shoulder and screamed and screamed and screamed at the very top of her lungs.

•   •   •

The girl Pete finally found had superb breasts. And no eye-shadow. That was very important—Pete didn't like eye-shadow. Linda Medellin had always had a big thing for eye-shadow. Come to think of it, maybe that was why he didn't like it.

The girl now, though, had no eye-shadow, as well as superb breasts. She was a natural redhead with skin like whipped cream.

Whee!

I'm in an orgy, he thought hysterically, easing the girl down upon a cushion in the middle of the floor. *All around me, people are making love furiously and fiercely.*

The girl, it developed, was a talker. She simply didn't shut up, just went on babbling away a mile a minute while the fun and games went on. The fun was fun, and the games were wild games, and the talk was at least appropriate.

"Oh this is good this is good this is good. Oh I love it don't you just love it isn't it great isn't it great just great I love it so much. Oh do it more do it more don't stop don't ever stop because the more you do it the better it gets. So good so good so good. So good I love it I love it the longer it lasts the more I love it go on and on and this is good and yesyesyesyesyesyesyes I love it so sosososososo much!"

Boom-da-da-da-da-da-da-da-doom.

Freddie Koans was having the time of his life. Oh, this new stuff, this drug, it cut the life out of pot. It cut pot sixteen ways.

He had never thrown a party quite like this one before. Never. This was far and away the best.

Boppa-do-da-do-da. Boppa-boppa-boom.

In one part of the room two men were making love simultaneously to a single girl. Both of them at once were touching her, stroking her, and finally both of them were making love to her.

Both at once.

Boppa-boppa-boppa-boom.

To make up for the two-men-and-one-woman combination, two women made love to a man in another part of the room. Two of them—doing unimaginable things to the man.

Boom-boom-boom.

Oh, many things were happening. Some things were happening that Freddie Koans had never seen before and other things were happening that he had never even heard about.

Fascinating things.

Boom-boppa-da-da-da-da.

Fascinating rhythm.

Boom-boppa-da-da-boom-boom.

The drum never stopped. The rhythm slowed down a little at one point and lost some of its complexity, but that was understandable—Fred Koans was playing the drum with only one hand.

The girl whom Peter Galton had rejected, the girl with the flabby breasts that were so very sensitive, had a tough time finding herself a partner. After Pete had discarded her she had decided that being bare-breasted was not enough, so she had removed all of her clothing. But by that time the games were going on already and she couldn't find a man.

But at last she found one.

He was, quite literally, a man in a gray flannel suit. He was fat and fortyish and sweating but he was a man, and this was enough. She helped him out of the gray flannel suit, kissed him in a special way and told him that if he didn't make love to her at once she would murder him.

He didn't need coaxing.

"But where?" he wanted to know.

"The floor, jerk. Where else, you stupid jerk? The ceiling maybe, jerk?"

"There's no room on the floor."

He was right, amazingly enough. They were in the middle of a row of churning bodies and they could not get free to a place where there would be room to make love.

"Where?" he asked again.

"Here."

"There's no room to lie down."

"So we don't lie down."

"Huh?"

"We stand up," she said. "We stand up, you jerk, you dumb stupid son of a bitch of a jerk. We stand up and we do something. Now."

"Is it possible?"

"You're damn right it is," she said.

Damn right it was.

•   •   •

The Professor was a happy man.

He had had a marvelous time with Joyce Kendall. He had had a good time, and then each of his apprentices in petty larceny had a good time, and then it had been waltz-me-around-again-Willie all over again. Now, the second of the two morons was getting a second turn, and the Professor was very proud of himself. Very proud and very happy and altogether quite satisfied.

Joyce Kendall had been even better than he had expected. And, tomorrow morning, when Joyce Kendall woke up and remembered just what she had done the night before, life would be magnificent. Poor girl, she would go through hell for days. Possibly for the rest of her life. She might even cut her throat.

The Professor smiled.

One of the Professor's apprentices emerged from the bathroom.

"She wants more," he said incredulously.

"Good," the Professor said.

"I got no more for her, man."

"That's all right," said the Professor. He walked into the other room. "There's a girl in the bathroom," he announced loudly. "She needs men. All the men who are interested."

Faces turned.

"I suggest you form a line," the Professor continued. "The girl's capacity is incredible."

The line began to form. Some men were not yet exhausted and the whole idea appealed to them greatly. Others joined the line simply because it was there. It was a nice line, not too long and not too short.

Peter Galton was at the end of it.

CHAPTER 7

Dawn was gray and ugly. Dawn came through a window, a trickle of light, a warmth to the air. Morning was a smudge on a whore's face, a broken tooth, a stench pervading all.

Pete Galton woke up in the middle of a bathroom floor. The room smelled of sex and sickness. Pete's head ached dully, a slow pain that was always there and never stabbing, never biting, never proving to him that he was alive. Just a pain. He opened his eyes warily and looked around. He looked at the filthy bathroom. Then he looked down and studied the girl beside him.

At first he was afraid that she might be dead. Then he saw that she was breathing, slowly but regularly, and he felt better. Not good, but better. He eased himself up from the girl, careful not to wake her, took a last look around the bathroom and then he went out into the other room.

The room was empty of people. It reeked of sex and sweat, of people, of lust. Clothes were scattered throughout the room, and they reminded Pete that he was naked. He looked around for the slacks and shirt he had worn but they were gone. He remembered what a mess they had been and wondered hazily why anybody would want them. He did manage to find some underwear that was his size and his own tennis shoes, but he couldn't find the rest of his clothing. It irritated him.

Then, unaccountably, he found that someone had abandoned a perfectly fine gray flannel suit. He tried it on and it fit. Then he found a white shirt to go with it and took off the jacket, put on the shirt, buttoned it, and put on the jacket once again. Why in the world had anybody left the suit behind? Hats get forgotten, umbrellas get left at parties, but suits?

And then he began to remember the party. All of it, from the beginning when he had walked through the door with Joyce Kendall on his arm, to the end, when he had unceremoniously passed out in the pleasant aftermath of intercourse with Joyce Kendall.

All of it.

And now, remembering it, it seemed impossible that all that he remembered could ever have taken place. He could not fully believe that he had done the things he now remembered doing, that he could have seen the things he now remembered seeing. He felt weak in the knees and looked for a place to sit down. He found a cushion and sat on it but that didn't help. He was nauseous now and he had to throw up.

He didn't run into the bathroom. He vomited square in the middle of the floor, his stomach doing a neat flip and turning itself inside-out, and then he turned away and sat down again. He felt a little better now.

What was the matter with him? How sick was he, how rotten inside, that he could have done the things he remembered doing?

You're no good, he told himself. *You're a pig. Rotten inside. No good at all.*

Now what was he supposed to do? He wanted to get out of the place, to take a cab back to his own apartment and try to forget what had happened. A cab? Sure, except what in hell was he going to use for money? His wallet had been in his pants pocket. His pants were gone. That was nice.

On a hunch, he checked the gray flannel suit, checked first the pants and the jacket. If the suit's owner had had a wallet, he had it no longer. But there were a few crumpled bills in a back pocket, a five and three ones, and that would get him home.

He stood up and started for the door. Then he remembered the girl and remembering her made him stop in his tracks and try to figure things out all over again.

In a sense, what had happened to her was his fault. He had brought her here, brought her unprepared for what was going to happen. In another sense, she had asked for it, had wanted to go with him wherever he wanted to take her, had asked no questions and made no conditions whatsoever.

Was she his responsibility? Was anyone, himself concluded, the responsibility of one Pete Galton?

It was hard to say.

He was shaky now and he needed a cigarette. There weren't any in the gray flannel suit, unfortunately, and he rummaged around the room hunting for a pack. He found several flip-top boxes, all sadly empty, and he nursed a deep loathing for the manufacturers of flip-top boxes. The damned things looked full when they were empty. It was frustrating.

There was one Lucky left in a crumpled pack and he salvaged it, straightened it out, and let it dangle out of his mouth. Then he made another search and found a match. He lit the cigarette and took a deep drag on it.

It helped.

The girl, Joyce Kendall. What, now, was he going to do with her? Leave her there?

He got a good mental picture of the girl waking up, alone, nude, in an empty and filthy loft in the middle of nowhere. Alone with memories of the night before, memories that couldn't be too pleasing to her. She wouldn't even be able to find her way home. Probably wouldn't want to go home anyway. Hell, she might even take a dive through the window.

You never could tell. He himself was sick enough at the memory of the night before, and he was a dissipated man, not an innocent girl. And he hadn't done *that* much—while she had played hostess to at least twenty men.

Christ.

Well, he decided, he didn't have a hell of a lot of choice in the matter. He had to take care of her and that was all there was to it. He had to get her dressed, somehow, and get her back to the apartment, somehow, and get her to bed. Alone.

Clothes first—because it simply wouldn't do to carry a naked woman through the streets of New York. It just might attract attention. Briefly he remembered a case he had covered as a reporter, a case that had attracted a hell of a lot of attention. It seemed there was this joker from Jersey who came to New York, hit a few bars and ran into an old buddy who insisted on taking him home for the night.

They sacked out, he and the buddy, and the next thing he knew, the buddy's wife was hitting him over the head with a frying pan and chasing him out of the house for no apparent reason. He had waited on the street, and then she had thrown down his sport jacket.

Nothing more.

So the cops found him out on the streets of Brooklyn, this joker from Jersey, dressed in a sport jacket and a pair of shoes.

Nothing else.

It had caused a stir. And it would cause even more of a stir if he tried to carry Joyce Kendall home in her birthday suit. So he had to find something for her to put on.

The only female clothing in the room consisted of undergarments. No dresses, no sweaters, no skirts, no blouses. There were plenty of bras, some padded, some small, some the size of shopping bags, and plenty of lacy panties. But that was all, and Joyce Kendall in bra-and-panties was just as attention-getting as Joyce Kendall stark naked.

On a hunch, he checked the bathroom. Her clothes were piled in the tub—which was lucky. He decided that it would be silly to try putting underwear on her. Blouse, skirt and shoes would have to do. But how did you put clothes on a naked girl without waking her up? And, if the girl woke up while he was putting clothing on her, what in hell was he supposed to say?

He lifted her by her shoulders and managed to slip the blouse under her. He got her arms into the sleeves and buttoned all of the buttons. Any other time he might have had trouble ignoring the perfection of her body, the slope of her thighs, the swell of her breasts. Now, with sexual activity of any kind the furthest possible thing from his mind, it was easy.

When he was in the process of pulling the skirt up over her thighs, her eyes blinked. He got a hand under her rump, lifted, and pulled the skirt the rest of the way.

And she woke up.

"Wha—"

"Everything's going to be all right," he said quickly. "I'm trying to help you. Finish getting dressed and come with me. That's right—fix the skirt. Fine. And tuck the blouse in. Here are your shoes. Slip them on. That's right, that'll do it. Now come with me."

He noticed that she was in a daze, which was just as well with him. If she started asking questions now he didn't know what in the name of God he would do. But she was too dazed to ask questions. She stood up on unsteady feet and staggered along with him, out of the bathroom, through the main room, down the stairs to the street. It was the same gray dull morning outside the loft as it had been inside. He wished he had another cigarette.

Together they walked to Third Avenue. He had to hold her so that she would not fall to the sidewalk, so he had his arm around her waist, but there was nothing remotely sexual about the whole thing. He could barely believe that last night he had made love to this girl, that the two of them had been incredibly stimulated, that she had screamed at him, shouted for him to do it to her. Nor could he conceive of himself doing what he had done. It was something that had happened ages ago, in another time continuum in another universe, and it had no bearing whatsoever on here and now.

Here and now was entirely different. Here and now he was a Boy Scout doing his good deed for the day, after which he could tie a knot in his neckerchief and feel good about life. She was the old lady he was helping across the street.

They reached Third Avenue and he hailed a cab. The driver gave them both a funny look, but a fare was a fare and he wasn't about to give anybody a hard time. They piled into the back seat and he gave the driver the address, telling him to hurry.

The driver hurried.

They got out of the cab at the corner of Gay and Christopher. He gave the driver two singles and told him to keep the change. He didn't care how big a tip he left. The money wasn't his, anyway—it belonged to the man in the gray flannel suit. He couldn't care one way or the other about it. He just wanted to get the girl home, give her a sedative and put her to bed.

The front door was locked and he didn't have his keys. He pressed a buzzer for one of the other apartments and the return buzzer sounded quickly. A woman stared at him as he steered the girl up the stairs. "Forgot my key," he explained quickly, not waiting around to see how the explanation went over.

She had her key in the pocket of her skirt. He opened her door for her and shoved her inside. She stood there, bewildered, waiting for somebody to tell her what to do or where to go, waiting for some instructions or other because, right now, she obviously did not have a mind of her own.

"Wait right here," he said firmly. "I'll be right back. Wait here."

He raced up the stairs to his own apartment. The door was unlocked as always and he charged inside, found the bottle of Seconal in the medicine cabinet, took two pills and ran downstairs again. He found a glass in her apartment, filled it with water and presented her with the glass of water and the two pills.

"Take these," he urged.

She popped the pills into her mouth and washed them down automatically with a swallow of water. She followed his instructions implicitly, and he had the strange idea that if he told her to open the window and step outside, she would do just that, never stopping to question his suggestions.

"Take off your clothes," he said.

She got undressed, not at all embarrassed about appearing nude before him, and he made her get into bed and drew the covers over her. He told her to close her eyes, then sat down in a chair and waited for her to fall asleep. The Seconal worked quickly and it was not long before her eyes stayed closed and her breathing regulated itself.

On a strange, slightly disturbing impulse, he walked to the side of the bed and looked down at her. Then, very suddenly he stooped over and kissed her cheek.

She woke up hours later, woke up coming out of a dream. She did not know what the dream was about, only that it was a bad dream and that it made her feel unhappy.

She opened both her eyes. She looked around vacantly and discovered that she was in her own apartment. What day was it? Thursday? She was supposed to be at work. And it was too late for work, much too late for work.

And then, all at once, she remembered.

The Professor. Stripping her clothes from her body, his hands reaching for her. She had wanted it and they had slipped down onto the bathroom floor and the tiles had been rough beneath her but she had not minded them.

Then other men.

So many other men.

Man after man after man.

She took a deep breath and let it out slowly. She couldn't believe it and yet she knew that it was true, that everything and more that she remembered was true, that it had happened, that it had happened to her, that no matter how fervently she attempted to deny its existence, that existence would be no less valid, that occurrence would be in no case erased.

She wanted to scream.

How could she have done it? What was wrong with her? She recalled her loneliness and her need and she wondered if these things had betrayed her. Or had there been something else? It seemed impossible that she could have been transformed into a sex maniac by the simple need for companionship, that her loneliness had changed her into a sex-hungry bitch who took on all comers on the bare scratchy floor of somebody's bathroom.

But—

It was too much for her. She heaved a sigh, then rolled over on her side and groaned.

And there was the man.

She didn't know his name, didn't recognize him, not exactly. She knew that she had seen him before, that he looked familiar, but her disorderly memory couldn't make all the connections that had to be made.

"Who are you?"

"Pete Galton."

The name, too, was familiar.

"Do I know you?"

"Yes."

"Then—"

He put out the cigarette he had been smoking. "Joyce," he said gently, "how much do you remember?"

Her face went red.

"I took you to a party," he said. "And I woke up and you were there. I brought you home."

"Did we—"

"Yes," he said. "We made love."

There was absolutely nothing to say to that. She looked at him and wondered what it had been like making love with him, wondered whether he had enjoyed it, wondered whether she herself had enjoyed it. It was impossible to remember, equally impossible to imagine. She was thoroughly lost.

"Pete—"

"Yes?"

"Tell me what happened."

"Don't you remember?"

"Some of it," she said. "It's all blurred. I don't understand it at all. I . . . would you explain it to me? As much as you know about it?"

His face darkened. "You remember some of it," he said. "Maybe that's enough."

"I don't understand."

"Maybe you know as much as you ought to know. Maybe it would be a good idea to forget the rest."

She shook her head. "No," she said. "No, that's no good. I want to know. Don't you see, Pete? I have to know what happened. I just have to know."

"Why?"

"Because I do."

"But why?"

"I just do," she said. "No matter what I did, it's better if I know about it. Please tell me."

He found another cigarette, put it to his lips, scratched a match and lit the cigarette. His eyes were troubled and she thought that perhaps he was right, perhaps she should leave well enough alone and forget the parts that she couldn't remember. But she couldn't do that. She had to know.

"Please tell me, Pete—"

"Joyce—"

"Please, Pete. I have to know."

"All right," he said slowly. "All right."

CHAPTER 8

She listened thoughtfully, her eyes on his rugged face, catching everything he said and not missing a word of it. Sometimes this was difficult because what he was saying embarrassed him and his voice would drop very low and his face would turn from her. But he kept talking and she kept listening and in this way she heard all of it.

Most of it, she had remembered. But now she learned something very important, something that reassured her, that made her realize that she was not a complete tramp. At least she hadn't been the only one, the whore in a roomful of virgins. If what he was saying was true, the party was a mob scene, an orgy, with dozens of men and women rooting around on the floor like animals in heat. That didn't make her own part any more attractive, but at least it helped take the burden of guilt from her shoulders.

And if what he said about the grape juice was true—and there was certainly no reason for him to be lying—then the fault was not hers at all. She remembered, vaguely, drinking a great quantity of the juice, glass after glass after glass, and shortly thereafter she had been in the bathroom, and then—

She relaxed. This didn't erase her guilt but it assuaged it considerably. It provided a reason for her actions, but her actions still remained, real and ineradicable. She would pass men on the street and wonder whether or not they had slept with her.

Or, worse, she would see a face on the lonely streets and re-member that the face had hovered over her, that the man's body had borne down upon her, taking its pleasure with her and giving pleasure to her.

That would be worse.

Only two men had known the secrets of her body before that night. Two men—then no one for well over a year. And now—

"Why did you help me?" she asked suddenly. "You could have left me there. Why did you bring me home?"

"I don't know," he answered honestly. "I woke up and you were there and I realized how messy it would be for you, waking up all alone and lost."

"It was very good of you."

He shrugged deprecatingly. "I'm always nice to stray cats and dogs," he said. "A real Boy Scout."

"But you were right. I'm glad you were there."

He smiled sadly.

"Did we . . . did you and I make love last night?"

"Yes."

She looked at him. He had turned his face away from her and she could not see his eyes. But she looked at him, at the lines of his face, and she realized that she was not embarrassed with him. Perhaps he knew too much about her, so much that embarrass-ment was out of the question. It was hard to say, but whatever the reason she could not conceive of herself blushing before him, or avoiding his eyes, or being overwhelmed with guilt when she was near him.

"Was it . . . good?"

"I don't know."

"Either it was good or it wasn't. Was I . . . active? Hungry for it? I was probably begging you, wasn't I?"

"Let's not talk about it."

She realized with a start that he was far more embarrassed by the discussion than she was, and this was something she could not fully understand. She opened her mouth to say something, then thought better of it and let the matter drop.

"What time is it?"

"A few minutes after six. Why?"

"God," she said. "I was supposed to go to work today. The whole day is shot now."

"Forget it."

"I would just be getting home now," she said. "After eight dull hours, I would just be getting home. That's funny, isn't it?"

"Is it?"

"I think so. Maybe they'll fire me. I didn't even call them up to tell them I wouldn't be coming in. They'll wonder what was wrong with me."

"I don't think they'll fire you. You can go in tomorrow and explain you were sick or something."

"But I could have phoned—"

"Tell them the phone was in the hall and you were too sick to go all the way to the phone. They'll understand. Better yet, stay home tomorrow and call them. That'll make it look better. Then you can have the weekend to rest up and when you come in hale and hearty on Monday morning, they won't suspect a thing. You can even carry a handkerchief and blow your nose in it every once in a while for effect."

She grinned. "You sound like an old hand at the game."

"What game?"

"Calling in sick. Did you do that this morning?"

"Hardly. I'm unemployed."

"Oh, I'm sorry."

"Don't be," he said. "I'm not."

She listened while he ran through his own history—the job and how he had left it and what he was doing now.

"You're a writer, then," she said finally.

"No."

"But—"

"I'm a bum," he said, correcting her. "A writer is somebody who writes. I don't do that. I haven't written a line in almost a week. I'm a bum, you see. I sit around and drink and smoke."

"Pretty soon you'll finish the book," she said confidently. "And then somebody will publish it."

"I doubt it."

"You don't think it'll sell?"

"I don't think I'll finish it," he corrected, smiling grimly. "As a matter of fact, I seriously doubt that I'll ever write another word of it."

"Why not?"

"I just don't feel like it."

"Then what will you do for money? Get another job?"

He laughed. "Not that, I'm afraid. Oh, I'll find some way to get by. If worst comes to worst, I guess I'll rent a loft over on the East Side and hold orgies."

For a second or two she wasn't sure how she was supposed to read to a line like that. Then, suddenly, the line seemed very funny and she resolved her dilemma by laughing. He joined in the laughter, his eyes warm when he looked at her.

"Look," he said finally, "it's dinner time and I'm pretty hungry. You must be starving yourself. When did you eat last?"

"Yesterday."

He sighed. "In that case, we better get you to a restaurant before you pass out again. I've got a fine idea. There's an Italian place around the corner with the best damned Neapolitan cooking in New York. We'll go there, have a glass or two of sour red wine, a heaping plateful of good food and then you'll feel a hell of a lot better. How does that sound?"

"It sounds great."

"Fine. I'll go up to my apartment and change while you get some clothes on."

"But—"

"But what?"

"You're unemployed," she said, "and you shouldn't have to spend money. Why not stay here? I'll whip up some supper and it won't cost us anything."

He grinned. "That's sweet of you. But it's time for a little education for you, Joyce. Unemployed and broke are not perforce synonymous. I won't have any money worries, not for a few weeks. Now, I'm going to run upstairs, change into something a little more comfortable than somebody else's gray flannel suit and locate my bankroll. Meanwhile, you get up, take a fast shower, get some clothes on and look pretty. I'll be down as soon as I can. Good enough?"

Her eyes stayed on him until he had left her apartment.

Strangely, inexplicably, she still wondered how it had been with them when they had made love.

Then she got out of bed, walked quickly to the bathroom and turned the shower on full blast. She took a very hot shower first, letting the water beat down on her and sting her soft skin. She rubbed the soap into her flesh, trying to wash away the traces of all the men of the night before.

Then she turned off the hot water, letting an icy spray lash her, closing up the pores, bringing her back to life. She stepped at last from the shower and rubbed herself dry with a towel. Back in the bedroom she dressed quickly—a pink sweater, a black skirt, a pair of brown loafers.

Then she sat on a chair in the living room and waited for him to came back to her. She hoped he would hurry. She was hungry now. And that was not all.

She wanted to see him.

Faraci's Kitchen was one of too few Village restaurants which managed to retain a luxurious sort of elegance without burdening their clientele with high prices. The booth Pete and Joyce shared was intimate, the light soft and diffused. The wine was sour and red and ice-cold. They drank it slowly and studied the menu carefully. When the waiter appeared, smiling, Pete ordered the lobster *fra diavolo* for her and the *calamari* for himself.

"What's *calamari*?"

"Squid," he told her.

"Squid?"

"Like octopus. Only smaller."

She made a face.

"It's good," he said. "I've ordered it in Philippine restaurants, too. The sauce is more gamy there. But I like the way the Italians cook it."

"I think I'll stick to the lobster," she said. "I'm not too squeamish but there's something about the idea of gobbling up a squid—"

"What's the difference? When you stop to think about it, a lobster isn't so pretty either. I mean—"

"Don't tell me," she interrupted. "You'll spoil it for me. I love lobster."

They drank wine and exchanged small talk while they waited for the food. It came and it was worth the wait. The lobster had been cooked expertly in a subtle sauce and it was delicious. He made her try a bite of his *calamari* and she was surprised to discover that it was very good.

She hadn't realized how hungry she was. The food disappeared in short order and he didn't have to twist her arm to get her to order a dish of tortoni for dessert. They capped the meal with cups of espresso then sat, contented and pleasantly filled with food, looking at each other.

The waiter, still smiling, brought the check. It came to only four dollars for the two of them. Pete gave him a five and waved away the change.

"Well," he said, "that does it. Come on—I'll take you home."

They walked back to Gay Street in silence. For some reason neither of them felt enough like talking to start a conversation going. They walked without speaking. Joyce had a strange urge to slip her hand into his, to hold hands with him. But she held herself back and they simply walked together.

He used his key on the front door and walked her up a flight of stairs to her door. "Well," he said, "I'll see you. You'd better take it easy, get some rest."

"You're going?"

He nodded.

"Where?"

"Jazz club a little ways away. I thought I'd drop by for a few sets. Nothing much else to do."

She hesitated. "Could I . . . come with you? Dutch, of course. I just don't want to sit around alone. Not tonight."

Now it was his turn to hesitate and she was sorry at once that she had asked. "Forget I said anything," she said. "It was stupid of me to horn in. You're meeting someone, aren't you?"

"No," he said, smiling. "No, nothing like that. I'd be happy to have you along. It's just that I thought maybe you ought to get some rest. You know, take it easy. You've had a pretty rough time of it, you know."

"I'm all right now. Besides, I slept all day long. And I'm not going to work tomorrow, remember? I'm taking your advice on how to con my employers."

"You sure?"

"I'm sure. Unless you don't want me along. Just tell me. I don't bruise too easily."

"I'd like your company," he said. "Let's go."

"Do I have to change?"

"Not for the Dime Note. It's an informal club. The tourists haven't found out about it yet. Let's go."

The music was hard bop—harsh, discordant, driving and furious. It was new to her—her ears had become more attuned to college boy jazz, West Coast harmonies and dance band drivel. But the more she listened to the music, the more she found herself in rapport with it. The trumpet snapped and squealed at her, the piano pounded complex chords that were never out of place, and after two or three numbers she was in tune with the music, fully able to relax and enjoy it. She did not understand it, not in the literal sense, but she liked what she heard.

She drank orange blossoms and he drank bourbon neat but neither of them did too much drinking. The club, a hole in the wall named the Dime Note, was designed for listening rather than for drinking. The waiter only came around between sets, unwilling to interrupt the music. Which was just as well with the intense people who occupied the tables and watched the musicians constantly, listening hard to every note.

The two of them did not talk while the group was playing. Between sets they talked a little, saying nothing in particular. It was an easy atmosphere that had developed between them. In one sense, there was no pretense, no secrets, nothing held back. They had already slept together, albeit under less-than-perfect conditions and still, at the same time, they had no strings on one another. They would relax and talk, and then the music would begin again and they would lose themselves in it.

A set ended.

"It's almost midnight," he said. "We'd better get going. It's late, even if you're not going to work tomorrow. You've had a busy time lately."

"I didn't realize it was that late."

"The time goes fast here. Let's go."

He insisted on paying the whole check. Then he took her arm and led her out of the club. It was a cool night outside—moonless and starless, with the streets strangely quiet. This time he took her hand automatically when they walked. Again they were silent. They walked slowly.

Then once again they were on Gay Street, in front of their building, and he was opening the door with his key. He led her inside and they walked up the flight of stairs, then stood in hazy silence in front of her door. She got her key in the lock, turned it and shoved the door open. Then she turned at the door, ready to say good-bye to him.

"I'll see you," he said. "Maybe I'll drop by tomorrow. If it's okay with you."

"Of course," she said.

"Well—"

"I had a very nice time tonight, Pete. It was good of you. The dinner and the music. I enjoyed it."

"We'll have to do it again soon."

"That would be nice."

"Well—"

"Pete?"

He looked at her.

"Pete, don't go. Please don't go."

He waited.

"Pete, stay with me. Tonight. Stay with me. I want you with me, Pete. I want you to sleep with me."

Silence.

"Are you sure, Joyce?"

"I'm sure."

"This isn't . . . necessary, you know."

"I know."

"I mean—"

"I know what you mean. I want you with me. I want you to make love to me."

His mouth opened but he didn't say anything.

Her heart was beating quickly and her mouth was dry. She didn't know how she might be sounding to him, whether she was acting like a woman or a tramp or a badly-frightened little girl. She didn't even care how it sounded. She knew only that she wanted him with her. That much was very important to her at the moment. Nothing else mattered.

"I want you here," she said. "Holding me in your arms. I want you next to me all night long. And I want you to be there in the morning when I wake up. Is that horrid of me?"

"No," he said slowly. "No, of course not."

"Would you like that, Pete?"

"Yes," he said gently. "I'd like that very much."

He took her face between his hands and brought it up close to him. His mouth found hers and they kissed—a gentle, strangely passionless kiss.

The bargain was sealed.

They walked inside the apartment. He closed the door, turned the bolt. Then he took her in his arms again and they kissed once more in the same manner.

"Do you like me, Pete?"

"Yes. Very much."

"Am I . . . all right?"

"You're sweet. You're very sweet."

"Do you want me?"

"Very much."

"Make love to me, Pete. Make love to me. But be gentle. Please be very gentle with me."

His arms went around her, holding her close. His lips brushed her cheek, then found her mouth again. His hands stroked her back gently and his lips on hers made a solemn promise of sweetness, of tenderness, almost of love.

CHAPTER 9

It was slow and gentle. There was no mad rush to the bedroom. It
proceeded in easy stages and she was thankful for that.

He kissed her, then led her to the couch and sat down beside
her. His hands were well-behaved. He did not try to rush anything. He kissed her again and again, gentle kisses, and when his
tongue pried her lips apart and sought the shelter of her mouth,
she was ready to receive him.

They exchanged long, deep kisses, his tongue stabbing far into
her mouth, probing and touching, finding her tongue and licking
it, touching her lips, her teeth, the roof of her mouth. Her arms
wound around him and she held him close.

He cupped her breast in one hand and she could feel the hand
through the sweater and the bra. He merely held her, not squeezing, not stroking, and the gentle pressure of his hand was just
what she needed. It made her feel safe, safe and comfortable. She
covered the hand with a hand of her own and held it tight against
her breast.

"You have beautiful breasts," he said. "You're a beautiful girl."

"Do you think so?"

"Yes."

He kissed her again. Now his hand contracted slightly and a
bolt of joy thrilled through her warm flesh. This was good, sweet,

perfect. She was glad that he was taking his time, being gentle with her, spending a great deal of time in the foreplay. It made everything much better.

"Lie down, Joyce."

She curled up on the couch and he stretched out beside her. The lights were on and she could see his face. His eyes were clear and calm, his mouth serious but not grim.

"Now, kiss me."

They kissed again. This time she took the initiative, sending her own tongue darting out between his slightly-parted lips.

It was good.

His hand slipped under her sweater, cool and sweet on her bare back. He rubbed her back and she relaxed, responding to the pressure of his fingers on her back. She lay back, motionless, submitting to the caress and enjoying it.

His hands freed the sweater from the skirt, pulled it up over her head. She helped him. Then his hands found her again, found her breasts, his touch more keenly felt now through the bra alone without the sweater to interfere with the sensations.

She arched her back and his hands went around her again, reaching for the bra clasp. He had a little trouble with it but then it was off and he was kissing her again. She felt his body pressing against her bare breasts. Then he released her and removed his own shirt, then took her once again in his arms.

The touch of his flesh against her was sweet, warm, delicious. Her arms were tight around him, holding him very close. Her whole body was starting to throb with desire. But it was a gradual desire, a clean desire, not the hot hoof-pawing itch of the night before. It was good and what they were doing was good and she was happy.

"Joyce—"

His hands were on her breasts now. They cupped the two large globes of succulent flesh, squeezing, stroking, inching ever so gently, coaxing unbelievable responses from her. She had trouble remaining still under his touch. She wanted to writhe, to squirm, to let her hips move instinctively in the age-old rhythms of love.

He took off her shoes, her socks. All the while he kept kissing her breasts, first one and then the other, and the excitement was a fever within her.

"Joyce—"

"Oh, this is good. This is so good."

He unclasped her skirt, unzipped it, and she raised herself up on her elbows so that he could pull it free from her. Then she lay on the couch while he stood up awkwardly, removed his trousers and stepped out of them. Then he was with her again, lying next to her on the couch, and she felt his body press against her own body.

"Do you like this, Joyce?"

"God—"

"And this?"

"Oh, I love it. I love it!"

He touched her some more, kissing her, stroking her, and then he moved away from her, lifting her from the couch with one arm under her thighs and the other beneath her back. He held her gently but firmly, carrying her without effort from the couch to the bedroom. He set her down tenderly on the bed and lay down beside her.

Then he began again, kissing her, touching her breasts, stroking the sweet beauty of her. Everything he did to her raised her passion to unbelievable heights and she knew that it had to happen soon, that he had to take her and make love to her in a hurry or she would begin to climb the walls, that she needed him more desperately than she had ever needed anything in her life.

It was different from the other night, completely and totally different. Before there had been the blind uncaring need induced by the drug, an insatiable desire that could be satisfied by any man. This was very different.

This was a lust, but a lust not for just any man. It was a lust for Pete, Pete Galton.

It began.

Their bodies locked in a tight and hot and eager embrace. She could feel the hairs on his chest against her breasts. His mouth was against her neck and his tongue was setting her throat on fire.

And their bodies moved in the rhythms of love, the ancient rhythms, making the movements that were as old as the earth, as old as the stars, as old and perfect as time.

Their sweat ran in little rivers that mingled and became indistinguishable. Their passion mounted at several times the speed of light. The world was theirs now, theirs alone, and it was good and sweet and beautiful.

"Pete—"

The night enveloped them in a blanket of love and the stars raced by them. The world turned on its axis and danced madly by. Time stopped and the stars turned out their lights.

"Pete, this is good. I need you, Pete. God, I need you. This is so *good!*"

Her heart raced at top speed. Her hands raced over his body. Her nails dug into his flesh and broke the skin.

And Heaven approached.

They worked together, reaching, straining, heading for Heaven. They built a palace of love and the world moved beneath them. Their hearts sang.

And then they reached Heaven, passed the gates of Heaven, passed the gates to Paradise together at the same incredibly perfect point in time.

And it was over.

They lay without speaking, lay motionless in the position of love, locked in love and too awed by it to say a word.

He woke up curiously content, strangely at peace with the world. All the marijuana, all the liquor, all the madcap sex—all these things had failed to supply what he had had that night with her. His mind reeled, trying to grasp the import of what he was learning about himself.

The liquor—alcohol bringing stupor, bringing oblivion, a palliative to sore nerves, to a mind that could not otherwise forget things that demanded to be forgotten.

Marijuana—a crutch for the mind, a crutch for the sick mind, letting its user make his own rules and bend them if he deviated from them.

Sex—also a crutch, a substitution of the idea of Woman for the particular woman who was desired.

All unnecessary now.

It had been Linda, Linda Medellin, who had made the alcohol and the marijuana and the depravity so essential. It had been the loss of Linda Medellin and the ineradicable memory of Linda Medellin and the insatiable desire for Linda Medellin which had brought the sickness to him, which had turned his world inside-out and which had replaced it with the brave new world of alcohol and marijuana and depravity, of sickness and hopelessness.

Now Linda Medellin did not matter at all. And Joyce Kendall was the only thing on earth that mattered.

He sighed contentedly. He turned to her now, to his woman, and he looked at her with happy eyes. The sheet had fallen away from her and she slept uncovered, beautiful in her nakedness. Her face was snuggled close to her pillow and her eyes were shut. Her body made one beautiful sensuous curve from the nape of her neck over her shoulder to her waist, up over hip and down over thigh.

She was beautiful.

He rested a hand on her shoulder, touching her. She made a sound but did not move.

He ran his hand over her body, not with passion but with love, thinking that this was his woman now, that this belonged to him, that this was his. He was not lost any longer and neither was she. Both of them had been alone, terribly alone, and now neither of them would be alone any longer. They had found each other and they needed each other and they belonged to each other and they would manage against the world no matter what happened.

He glanced at the clock. It was almost nine o'clock and at nine she ought to call in to her employers, to tell the illustrious people at Armageddon Publications that she was sick, that she would not be able to come in until Monday.

It was time to wake her.

He touched her more, his hands gentle, and she opened her eyes and looked at him lovingly. Her arms opened for him and he came to her, thinking that she could call a few minutes late if she had to. Some things were more important than a phone call, more important than a job.

This was one of them.

It was slow and sleepy. It was warm and sweet.

It was the beginning and the end of the world.

It was very good.

"Mrs. Evans? This is Joyce Kendall. Yes, that's right. Mrs. Evans, I'm afraid I won't be able to come in today. Yes, I know. I wanted to call you yesterday but couldn't. No . . . you see, there's no phone in my apartment and the doctor told me to stay in bed. I'm not sure just what it is. The flu, he said, but I guess that can mean almost anything. Yes, that's right. I'll be in Monday if I can. I feel a little better today and I think I'll be able to make it Monday. I hope so. Yes, I will. Thanks very much, Mrs. Evans."

She grinned and replaced the phone on the hook. "Well?" she demanded. "How was I?"

"You lie perfectly."

"Did I sound nervous? I was, you know. I was sure she'd see right through me."

"People generally believe what they want to believe. There's nothing to worry about."

"I know," she said. "But I can't help feeling guilty about it. After all—"

"After all," he cut in, "they pay you a lousy fifty bucks a week and work your fingers off. You don't have to feel sorry for them. You've been getting the wrong end of the stick all along. They won't miss you for two days."

"I suppose not."

"So there's nothing to worry about. Want to go out now and have some breakfast?"

"I've got a better idea," she said. "Suppose I bring you breakfast in bed."

"You just did. Remember?"

She giggled. "You know what I mean."

"Of course. And you know what I mean."

She giggled again. "Cut it out," she said. "Quit touching me like that. Do you know what you're doing to me?"

"Tell me about it."

"Pete! God! Now listen to me for a minute, will you?"

"I'm listening."

"And quit doing that to me."

He sighed.

"I'm going to cook breakfast for you," she said. "How do pancakes sound?"

"They sound delicious."

"Pancakes and maple syrup. And bacon. How do you like your bacon?"

"Crisp."

"And your coffee?"

"Black, no sugar."

"Orange juice first?"

"Sounds great."

"Well, you better quit doing that or you won't get anything."

"Not anything at all?"

"Pete! Now let go of me. I have to go cook. You sit here and, and . . . well, read a book or something. Okay?"

"Oh, all right."

She got away from the bed, slipped on a robe and went in to the kitchenette. She mixed milk and eggs and pancake mix in a bowl and lined a pan with bacon.

While she cooked the food and poured two glasses full of fresh orange juice and put a pot of coffee on the stove, she thought about Pete and about herself. She was genuinely happy now for the first time in a long time. For once something had happened completely without her planning it and it had been perfect.

And she knew that everything would be perfect from now on. Everything.

They would live together. That was as much as she knew. They would live together and they would be happy together and that was all that mattered. She wondered whether they would be mad at her at her job and she decided that she didn't care. As long as she and Pete were together, they would be all right. It was that simple. They had each other and they were set that way.

She brought in the orange juice first. Then she carried in two plates, with the pancakes drowned in real maple syrup and the bacon crisp and delicious. He started in on the food while she poured two cups full of coffee and brought them in.

"Hey," he said. "You didn't tell me you could cook. You should have told me before."

"You didn't ask me."

"There must have been other things on my mind. Seriously, this is delicious."

"It's not really too tricky," she said. "Any damned fool can make pancakes and bacon."

"Maybe," he said. "But everything got ready at the same time. That's the surprising thing."

"It is?"

"It certainly is. When I cook, you see, everything turns out pretty well. Considering."

"Considering what?"

"Considering I don't cook too well. But that's not the main thing. The main thing is that I have to eat in stages. Take this breakfast, for instance. First I would have poured a glass of orange juice, and I would drink the orange juice, and then cook pancakes, and pour maple syrup over them, and eat them. Then I'd fry the bacon, and eat the bacon. Then I would heat up some water and make a cup of instant coffee. And drink it."

"It's better when it all gets done together."

"It is," he said.

"So you like the way I cook?"

"I like the way you do everything."

"Want to give me a hand—"

"I'd love to."

"That's not what I meant! Oh, God! Stop that now! I meant with the dishes."

"Oh," he said. "Well, sure."

•   •   •

When the dishes were done and put away they sat on the couch and drank more coffee. It was a lazy day, unhurried and calm, warm but not too warm. She felt very close to him. The intimacy of getting up together, eating breakfast together, washing dishes together and sitting together over coffee was equally as important as the intimacy of the bed.

It was an intimacy she had shared with no other man. With Joe lovemaking had been an end unto itself. Their love, such as it was, was a thing of backseats and motels. With Pete the relationship, brief as it was so far, was full and complete. Their minds were together just as their bodies had been together. Nothing was hidden, secret.

"What next?" she wondered aloud.

"For me?"

She nodded.

"I don't know," he said honestly. "I suppose I'm back in the real world now. No more bumming around. I don't know."

"You're not going to get your old job back, are you? With the newspaper?"

"I don't think they'd have me if I wanted to come back. But I don't want to anyway. Newspaper work was fun while it lasted. I don't think it would be fun any more."

"Will you finish the book?"

He shrugged. "Maybe. I don't know. I can hardly remember what I've written so far. I haven't touched it in days. And it's not the sort of book you can sit down and finish. It just rambles, sort of. I don't know if I'll ever finish it."

He turned to her. "What about you? You're going back to Armageddon, aren't you?"

"I think so."

"To be a first reader. That's pretty funny when you stop to think about it."

"How?"

"Sitting in judgment at Armageddon. See?"

"Uh-huh. I've got an idea."

He looked at her.

"What kind of writing have you done? I mean outside of the book and the newspaper work."

"Not a hell of a lot. A couple articles here and there. Nothing much else. Why?"

"I was just thinking." She took a cigarette from him and let him light it for her. "Do you think you could do some magazine stuff? Stories or articles?"

"Maybe."

"Then I could sit in judgment on them."

"You mean I should write for Armageddon?"

"Why not?" She smiled. "I could let you know just what they were looking for, bring home magazines for you to study. Then you could submit them and I'd pass them on. I wouldn't be much help to you, not really, but at least you'd get past the first reader. That might be something."

He closed his eyes and thought it over. "I don't know," he said at last. "I don't know."

"Wouldn't you want to do it?"

"I'm not sure. It'd beat working, that's for sure. But that's not the point."

"What's the point?"

He shrugged. "It's not easy," he said. "Writing garbage well is tougher than writing good stuff. I've tried and I know a little about it. It's not easy."

"You could do it."

"I'm not sure I could. Even if I could, it's a hell of a tenuous existence. No weekly paycheck to brighten your Fridays. Some weeks no money comes in. Then what do we do?"

"We live on hamburger."

"You make it sound easy. It's not that easy, Joyce. I've known a few writers. One guy was doing pretty well, hitting the slicks from time to time. He wrote articles. He did that for three years, did pretty well at it, and then dropped it all and went back to work on a newspaper for less dough than he'd been making free-lancing. Said he didn't like the pressure, the uncertainty of the whole thing. In the newspaper business he had money coming in all the time. Nothing to worry about."

"Maybe he was afraid," she suggested.

"How do you mean?"

"Afraid to take a chance. Afraid to do anything unless it was all planned out for him. I've been like that, Pete. Gutless. Afraid to gamble."

"You?"

"Me. My life is so well-ordered it's sickening. At least it used to be. Now it's changed."

"For the better?"

"God, yes! Listen to me, Pete. I think you could do it. I mean, we could do it. I'd be giving you a hand, remember. I'd know what they were looking for, the length and everything, and that would make it easier. Don't you think?"

"Maybe."

"And if it works," she went on, "then it would be worth it. Then you would work when you wanted to work and we could be together when we wanted to be together. Wouldn't that be good?"

"Sounds great," he admitted.

"And you can do it. I'm sure you can, Pete. Some of the magazines are always hungry for material. The confessions especially. Why, they—"

"That crap."

"So what? Pete, they pay three cents a word. And they don't care whether or not the author is well-known because the stories run without by-lines anyway. Suppose you do a five thousand word story. That's about twenty pages or so. You'd get a hundred and fifty dollars."

"For twenty pages?"

"About that."

"I could write that in a day," he said. "If I could think of anything to write about."

"You'd think of something."

He frowned. "You know," he said, "it just might work out. Damn it, it just might."

"Is it worth a try?"

"Sounds like it."

"Monday," she said. "Monday I'll go to work and bring home a batch of magazines. Then you can read them and study them and start hitting the typewriter. It'll take a while before the stuff starts getting good. But we can manage."

"We can eat hamburger."

"Right." She smiled. "Now shut up," she said. "And kiss me."

He kissed her.

He kissed her again.

"Confessions," he said. "The world's worst garbage. Sin, suffer and repent. That's the formula, isn't it?"

"More or less. There are a few switches, I think, but that's the basic idea."

"Shouldn't be too tough," he mused. "Sounds like one hell of a drag but it shouldn't be too tough. Matter of fact, part of it might be fun."

"Which part?"

"The sin part, silly. What else?"

"I wouldn't know," she said. "I'm afraid I don't know anything about sin."

"You don't?"

"Nope."

"Like hell you don't," he said. "You could give lessons."

"Honestly?"

"Honestly."

"Mmmmmmmmm," she said. "That's nice. It makes me feel wicked."

"You like to feel wicked?"

"Uh-huh. It's fun being wicked with you."

He kissed her again. This time his arms wrapped around her and she could feel faint stirrings of passion.

"Monday," he said softly. "Nothing to do until Monday. How are we going to kill time?"

"Don't you know?"

"Tell me about it."

"Guess."

"I can't guess."

She stood up, a faint smile on her lovely face. Her eyes were sparkling.

"Pete," she cooed, "I'll race you to the bedroom."

CHAPTER 10

My heart throbbed when I looked at him. How could I have done such a horrible thing? I didn't understand myself. I didn't know what was wrong with me. My mother's advice sounded in my ears and I realized how wrong I had been not to listen to her. I had been wrong, and now I would pay the price . . .

He put down the magazine and sighed. He ought to get paid three cents a word just for reading this tripe, he decided. Much more of this and he would go out of his mind. The stuff wasn't written, that was for sure. Nobody on earth could write such drivel. The editors obtained it by placing a hidden microphone in the washroom of a girl's reformatory.

It was Monday night. He was in his own apartment, dutifully plowing through the stack of confession magazines that Joyce had brought to him. She had come home from work smiling happily and she had handed him the pile of rubbish with the air of one making an offering to the gods.

He had grinned, accepting the magazines, and they had celebrated his success in advance with a meal at a steak house on Eighth Street complete with a drink before and a brandy after. Now she was downstairs in her own apartment and he was alone with the trials and tribulations of a hundred working-class girls.

It was terrifying.

He'd already finished two of the magazines. He skipped the articles, the letters-to-the-editor and the novelettes, sticking to the short pieces. He also avoided reading the one male-viewpoint piece in each issue, deciding that it made sense to concentrate on the greatest possible market.

And what a mess that market was.

Sighing heavily, he picked up the magazine and forced his eyes back to the story. It was a real lemon, primarily concerned with a young girl's loss of virginity, ensuing pregnancy and eventual reformation. It was amazing the way the confession mentality and morality worked. A girl could do it once in her life, standing up, at the worst time of the month, and she would still get pregnant. All the girls in confession stories got pregnant—except for the married ones, who wrote touching things entitled WE DO IT AND DO IT AND I STILL CAN'T GET KNOCKED UP, or something along those lines. It was frightening.

He finished the story, hoping against hope that the girl would fall off a cliff and make everybody happy. Then he lit another cigarette and moved on to the next story. He was reading with the twin aims of finding a repeating plot-pattern and absorbing the excruciatingly vile style in which all the stories seemed to be written. The second part seemed easy. All you had to do, he reasoned, was write exactly as the stupid readers would write if they knew how. You avoided letting the English language get in the way of the drivel you were trying to expound, and you kept things moving along simply but steadily.

The plot part was tougher. After he had finished the fourth magazine he sat back in his chair and closed his eyes, trying to think of a plot. The harder he thought, the more he realized the impossibility of what he was trying to do. Either a plot was so trite that it read like a carbon of every story in every magazine, or else it was so off-trail that it didn't fit the confession formula at all.

There didn't seem to be any in-between.

Hell, he thought, the idiots who wrote the stories had managed. They couldn't be such mental giants. If they were that brilliant, they wouldn't be wasting away at three cents a word. If they could do it, so could he.

Maybe.

With a sigh he abandoned the problem of plotting for the time being. The very next day, he decided, he would get up in the morning, sit down at the typewriter and pound out five thousand words of drivel. For the time being he would read and let everything soak in. After all, he thought, Rome wasn't built in a day. Or, as the anarchists put it, Rome wasn't sacked in a day either. He had plenty of time.

She had been reading when she heard the knock at her door. She marked her place, put the book down on a table and walked to the door.

"Who is it?"

"Tessie Trueheart," he said. "Girl Confessor. Leading hopeful scribe of the twentieth century."

She opened the door. He came inside and gave her a quick kiss and she stepped back, studying his face.

"How is it going?"

"Hard to say," he said. "I've never read such a heap of unadulterated ratcrap in my life."

"Bad?"

"That's about the smell of it."

"If you think that's bad," she said, "you should see the stuff I read and send back."

"Worse?"

"Much worse."

He shook his head. "I don't know how I'm going to work it, Joyce. They're all the same and they're all lousy. Every last one of them."

"Naturally. They're supposed to be lousy."

"Yeah, but—"

"You can manage," she said. "Done for the night?"

"Done until tomorrow. Know what I'm going to do tomorrow?"

"What?"

"I'm going to write one of the damned things," he said. "If it kills me, I'm going to write one of them. It'll be lousy and it won't sell but it'll be the first one. Then the next one'll be that much easier. It's a step."

"Good."

He scratched his head. "You know," he said, "I sure as hell *ought* to be able to grind this stuff out. Say, do people actually read this stuff?"

"Lots of them."

"Did you?"

"When I was in high school. Not all the time the way some

of the girls did, but often enough. I think everybody does. Didn't you read garbage?"

"Sometimes. Nothing like this, though."

"That's 'cause you were a boy," she said logically, "and I was a girl There's a difference."

"No kidding. Listen, when you read this stuff, did you believe it was all true?"

"Of course. Everybody does."

"God in heaven," he said.

"That makes it easier," she went on. "When you're writing it, I mean. It doesn't have to make sense the way good fiction does. It just has to tell a story. If it's factual, the reader can't be as critical as if it's fiction."

"I get it."

"So," she said, "tomorrow you grind out a story. And I put in eight hours at Armageddon. And we see what happens."

"In the meantime," he said, beautifully without preamble, "let's go to bed."

"Oh."

"After all," he went on, "I've put in a hard day's work reading rubbish. Now it's time for a little relaxation."

"Well," she said, "I'm afraid . . . that is—"

"Hey! You're not in the mood?"

"Oh, no," she said uncomfortably. "I wouldn't say that. I mean, I'm in the mood, all right. If I were any more in the mood I'd be dangerous."

"Then what gives?"

"Well, it's hard to say."

He stared at her.

"Let me put it this way," she said. "You are not going to be a father. Not for a while, anyhow."

"Oh."

"It happens," she said. "I mean, it happens. It could be worse. It could not happen and then where would we be?"

"Looking for an abortionist," he said. "Either that or knitting tiny garments. But it's a hell of a note."

"You said it."

"The trouble with you," he added, "is that you've been doing the wrong kind of reading. As an adolescent, I mean. You were reading confession magazines."

"So?"

"They tell you what not to do," he said. "You should have been reading something to tell you what to do."

"I don't get it."

"The ways of love," he explained, "are strange indeed."

"You mean—"

"I mean there are ways and ways."

"But—"

"Since you're teaching me how to write confession stories," he said, "it's only fair that I also assume certain professorial duties. You teach me things and I teach you things. Right?"

"Right."

"So," he said, "I've had my lesson for the day, and it's about time you had your lesson. If you feel in the mood, that is. If not, we can wait for a more appropriate time. There's no sense forcing knowledge upon an unwilling pupil."

She leaned toward him and rubbed her big breasts against his chest.

"If I were any more willing," she said, "I'd be giving you lessons. Let's go."

She was a good pupil and he was an excellent teacher. At one point the excitement was too much for her to bear and she screamed his name at the top of her lungs, screamed so loud she feared the roof would cave in.

They had no trouble sleeping that night.

In the morning he awoke when she did. She cooked breakfast, then when she went off to work, he went upstairs to his own apartment and locked himself inside. He stacked the confession magazines neatly in a corner, rescued his typewriter from where it had remained so long untouched, took it from the case and put it on the table. He stacked paper on one side, second sheets on another side, and put a piece of carbon paper between a good sheet and a second sheet, rolling the paper sandwich into his typewriter.

His fingers were stiff from so long without typing. He didn't know what to write or where to begin. He sat for a few moments without doing anything. Then, in the upper left-hand corner of the paper, he typed:

Peter Galton
21 Gay Street
New York 14, New York

He studied that for a few seconds, decided it looked fine, and typed a title halfway down the page:

I WAS BLIND TO HIS LOVE

He looked at that for awhile also, decided it looked just like every title in every confession magazine, and took a deep breath. Then he began to type:

It started out just like every other day. I got up in the morning, took a shower and brushed my teeth, ate breakfast and went off to work. I thought it would be the same as every other day, but I was wrong. I was all wrong . . .

The story went along like half-a-dozen others he had read. The girl who was supposed to be telling the story was fresh out of high school, working her fingers to the bone as a file clerk in a lawyer's office. A clown who went to high school with her is making a heavy play for her, but he's an ugly goof and she doesn't want to be seen with him. She's the type who places a great premium on physical attractiveness, and while she sees the clown from time to time, she is sure she can never feel anything for him.

And at the same time, she's got a big thing for the lawyer she's working for. He's a good-looking gent and she makes a hot and heavy play for him. He takes her out a couple of times and before long the two of them are in the rack together. He's got a wife, of course, and when she starts talking about marriage he tells her it's been fun but she should kindly get lost.

Which sort of breaks her up.

And, to make a long story short, which he was very careful not to do, she discovers that the ugly guy is a nice guy whereas the good-looking one was a one-eyed sonofabitch. She and Ugly get married, and although he's homely as sin to the rest of the world, he's the handsomest man in the world to her because of his inner beauty and because of the love for her that shines night and day in his stupid eyes.

Trash.

It went slowly, somewhat along the lines of pulling teeth. At times he would sit for minutes searching for the right word, and at other times his fingers chattered on the keyboard, pounding out a page in a matter of minutes. He kept a pot of coffee on the stove, pouring coffee into his stomach and pounding the typewriter until his arms ached.

The closer he got to the end, the tougher it became. It was trash, of course, and it was illogical, of course, and trying to tie the ends together with a pretty pink ribbon was something of a chore. But he kept writing, working furiously, kept prodding himself along with black coffee, and by the time Joyce got home from the office the story was finished and proofread.

"You did it," she said. She made it sound as though he had just discovered the wheel.

"Well," he said, "I wrote five thousand ill-chosen words. Let's leave it at that."

"May I read it?"

"Let's have dinner first," he suggested.

"I'm too excited to eat."

"We'd better eat now. After you read this you probably won't feel like eating. It's pretty horrible."

"Come on downstairs. I picked up a couple filets at the butcher around the corner. Sound good?"

"Delicious," he said. "Let's go."

The steaks were good. After dinner he solemnly handed her the script and did the dishes while she read it.

"Good title," she said immediately.

"That's all that's good."

"Shut up," she said reasonably. "I'm reading."

He finished the dishes about the same time she finished the story. "Well?" he demanded. "Horrible, wasn't it?"

"Not really."

"No?"

She took a breath. "If it came to my desk," she said, "I'd pass it on to the editor."

"You're kidding. Even if you didn't happen to be sleeping with the author?"

She nodded. "I'd still pass it on," she said, "but I have a hunch he'd reject it."

"Why?"

"Your plot's fine," she said, "but the structure's a little off. I'm no expert, honey, but—"

"Go on."

"Well, there's too much narration. You keep telling the story instead of showing it. See what I mean?"

"Not exactly."

She thumbed through the script. "Here," she said. "This

section, where she has the affair with the boss. It's almost all straight narration. Now, if you made the strictly narrative parts more of a summary and made one or two big scenes out of the most exciting part of it, it would be better. More of a story and less of a dry sermon."

"Oh," he said. "I get it."

"And the opening," she said. "It starts slow. If you start in the middle of a scene and then fill in with a re-cap later on, you'd do better."

He looked at her appreciatively. "You ought to write these," he said. "You're okay."

"I couldn't write them."

"Why not?"

"I can't write," she said simply. "I can look at something and get a fairly good idea what's good about it and what's wrong with it. You know, I'm getting so I even enjoy working at Armageddon. It's an enjoyable job once you get the swing of it. These past two days have been fun. But I could never write anything. I don't have the imagination."

"Like hell you don't."

"I mean when it comes to writing. Not what you're thinking. I could never come up with a plot, not the way you did."

"Quite a plot. A real honey."

"It's not bad."

"It's a sweetie. I'm another Shakespeare."

"Shakespeare didn't write confessions. The art form wasn't around then. He had to write plays."

"Well, thank God for that."

She sighed. "You're impossible," she said. "Do you want to do the revision? I think it'll have a good chance if you do."

"I'll go to work right now."

"Like hell you will," she said. "Tomorrow is soon enough. There's a good movie at the Waverly on Sixth—I noticed it coming home from work. Feel like a movie?"

"Maybe. What's playing?"

"*A Sound of Distant Drums*. It's supposed to be good."

"What the hell," he said. "It must be better than *I Was Blind To His Love*. Let's go."

Revision, he discovered the next day, was harder than writing it properly the first time. The rewrite he had to do was a pretty comprehensive one and he had to start from scratch. He was sorry now that he had bothered making a carbon of the first draft, but he had better things to worry about.

At least he knew where he was going. But now every word had to be weighed very carefully, every scene had to be built just right. He took his time, working slowly. Occasionally he would hit a section that could be copied almost verbatim, but those were the exceptions. Most of the copy needed a thorough overhauling.

This time, however, he was getting a good idea of what made a story tick. Now the story was taking a definite form and the form was soaking through to him. Strangely enough, it was beginning to make sense. The story had a beginning, a middle and an ending. It was too pat to be real, of course, and it was trash and bad trash at that, but the scenes formed a continuous chain of events and the people had a little substance to them.

He finished it and proofed it. And, amazingly, he found himself proud of what he had written. It was lousy, but at the same time it was pretty good, pretty damned good. It might sell and it might not but even if it didn't, he had proved something. He had written a story to fit the needs of a market and he had done a relatively good job of it.

While he waited for Joyce he sat around glowing. After part of the glow had worn off he picked up another confession magazine, one he hadn't gotten to yet, opened it at random and read a story. He saw that the story was better than his, that the organization was superior and that the plot was woven tighter than his. This disappointed him but at the same time he was glad that he was able to see what made one story better than another. This meant that he was getting a professional outlook, that he was learning the market.

Then he read another story. This one filled him with elation, because he saw that his story was visibly superior to this one, better plotted, better constructed, better written. It made him quite proud of himself.

When Joyce came home he was waiting for her, script in hand. "You can read this one before dinner," he said. "Tell me what you think of it."

He sat on the edge of his bed while she read the script. He watched her face as she read, watching every smile and frown and trying to guess why she was frowning or smiling. It seemed to take her forever to finish. Then she looked up from the script and he waited for her to say something.

"This is very good, Pete."

His heart jumped. "You mean it?"

"I mean it."

"Will it sell?"

"I think so. I'll take it in tomorrow and pass it on to Sheila Robbins. She's the editor of the two confessions. I'll tell her it just came in and I think it's good."

"How long will it take before she decides?"

She shrugged. "It depends on how much work she has. Submissions have been pretty slow lately, as far as I can gather. We'll probably hear next week at the latest."

"And you think she'll buy it?"

"I hope so. Of course, if she doesn't, it doesn't mean the story isn't any good. It might be just because she just bought another one that's similar to it. This one will sell somewhere, Pete. I'm sure of it. If she bounces it we'll submit it somewhere else."

He nodded.

"Now let's go downstairs," she said. "I'm starving. You must be pretty hungry yourself?"

"From what? Pounding a typewriter?"

"Uh-huh. Come on."

He followed her downstairs, curiously elated. He wondered if she was right, if the story would sell. If it did, that would be a hundred and fifty dollars. He—*they*—could use the money.

More than that, it would be a beginning.

CHAPTER 11

The next morning, when Joyce went to work, Pete decided to take a slight vacation. What the hell, he decided. He'd been working like a Turk for two days and in that time he'd managed to turn out a story. That was enough. Now he had a right to relax—take a stroll around the Village, have a beer or two. There was no sense driving himself nuts.

He tried to fall back into the mood. He walked over to Sheridan Square, crossed Seventh and wandered through the West Village. He came back over Bleecker to Macdougal and turned north. He let his eyes wander over the people and the buildings, and something strange happened.

He wasn't enjoying himself.

Somehow it wasn't enough any more—the same buildings, the same people, the same leisurely walks with no objective in mind, no real point to the journey. He wondered what was the matter. He went to Washington Square and picked out a comfortable spot on a comfortable bench but even the relaxed atmosphere of the park turned out to be furiously boring. He couldn't sit still, couldn't let the mood of calmness carry him off. After five minutes he couldn't stand it any longer. He got up from his bench and headed back toward his own apartment.

Now, on the way back, his mind began to churn at an

incredible pace. He walked blindly, letting the wheels in his mind turn over and over, and when he was back at his building and upstairs in his apartment he went at once to the typewriter, moving like an automaton, a robot. He sandwiched a sheet of carbon paper between a first and second sheet, rolled the result into the typewriter, and typed quite mechanically and automatically:

Peter Galton
21 Gay Street
New York 14, New York

Then he began to write.

The title he used was MY LIES WOULD SEND HIM TO JAIL, and the story moved more rapidly and surely than I WAS BLIND TO HIS LOVE. He was more sure of himself now, far more sure of his style and his plotting, and still more deeply aware of the basic nature of the medium in which he was working. The typewriter clacked steadily, the pages followed one another from blank stack to typewriter to completed stack, and the story forged onward.

It was about a girl out on a date with her own true love, who, in her own ill-chosen words, "went the limit." She was scared stiff, of course, and so was the guy, and there they were, parked on the side of the road waiting for an avenging angel to strike them dead with a bolt of lightning.

The avenging angel appeared in the form of a teenage hood on the lam from a reformatory he had just busted out of. The young hoodlum yanked open the door of the car, held a knife against the throat of the kid who had just finished boffing the girl, and made them drive him where they were headed. Meanwhile the police had a roadblock set up, which the hood tried to crash without a hell of a lot of success. There was a loud noise and broken glass and the next thing she knew she was waking up in a hospital.

There they told her a few sweet things—that her true love was dead as a lox, for example, and that they would start prosecuting the hood for rape immediately. They had examined her, put two and two together once they saw she was pregnant, and decided that Hoodie Boy must have done the spadework.

That left the heroine on the horns of an ugly dilemma. If she let them prosecute the little bastard for rape, then she wouldn't have to go into any long-winded explanations about the brat in her belly. If she didn't, she was in trouble. But how could she let Hoodie Boy go to jail for something he hadn't done? Somehow it just plain didn't seem fair to her.

Eventually she managed to straighten up and fly right, changing her testimony so that the clown was freed of the rape charge. That left him with nothing between himself and freedom, nothing but third-degree assault, manslaughter, kidnaping and a few other choice charges. More important, it left our girl Sunday at peace with the world. She was still knocked up, of course, and she would have to have the kid. But now she could live with herself.

He finished the script in record time, then read it over and proofed it. He firmly decided that if he ever met a girl with the fundamental philosophy of the one about whom he had just finished writing, he would break her neck and use her for fish bait. How phony could you get?

At the same time, while he was filled with contempt for the whole tone of the story he had just finished writing, he was pretty well pleased with the script itself. The plot was intricate enough to go over well in the confession field. The writing held up and the tone was consistent.

The story ought to sell.

The funny thing was that what pleased him most was how the story had come to be written. He hadn't planned on writing at all. He'd been going to goof off and instead, he had wound up typing away like a maniac. It was uncanny. Maybe he had found his niche in life—maybe he was doomed to end out his days on earth as a prolific writer of confession crap. If somebody had told him that a while ago he would have laughed. Or vomited. But now the idea didn't sound that bad at all.

He lit a cigarette and started pacing the floor, wondering what Joyce was doing and what time she might be home. The night before they had gone to a chamber music concert at one of the larger Village coffeehouses, then home and to bed. In the morning she made breakfast for the two of them, then grabbed up his script and headed for the office with it. Of course she wouldn't have any word yet, that much he knew, but he wanted to see her, to boast of writing another story so soon after the first, to have her read it and tell him what she thought of it.

More than that, he simply wanted her around. Having her around was good for him, very good indeed. He knew with complete certainty that he never would have tried writing again if it hadn't been for her. It wasn't just that she had suggested it, had picked up a pile of magazines for him and had prodded him into getting to work in the first place. It was more than that.

She had given him an incentive. Now he wanted to succeed, to make her proud of him, and he wanted to succeed so that the two of them could have more money to do the things they wanted to do. He knew what they were going to do the minute a story sold. First a pair of top sirloins at a good steakhouse, and then two seats front and center for the best show on Broadway, and then a pair of drinks someplace expensive on Central Park South, and finally a ride in a hansom cab through Central Park in the small hours of the morning. Not because he would enjoy doing these things, although of course he would, but because she would enjoy them. He wanted to do the things that would make her happy.

It had been so good for the two of them that it took effort now to remember what his life had been like before he had met her. The man he remembered was a very different man from the one he was now. A smaller man, for one thing. A man with no drive, no feeling—a man whom he found himself disliking intensely. There was no question about it—he had changed mysteriously into a much more pleasant individual since he had met Joyce Kendall.

Joyce.

He wondered just where they were going, just what would happen between them. He tried to visualize a break-up of the relationship they enjoyed, but such a break-up was totally impossible to picture. They were so close and they gave so much to each other that it was inconceivable that they should ever separate.

He thought about her—her face, her eyes, her body—and he waited for her, hoping she would get back soon.

"Pete!"

She was wearing a plaid skirt and a yellow blouse and she

looked very lovely. Her face was scrubbed and there was no lipstick on her lips.

She came to him, running into his arms and burying her face against his chest. She rubbed up against him, then raised her face for a kiss. His arms folded around her and he kissed her, grinding his lips almost painfully against hers, holding her close and kissing her quite thoroughly.

"Pete, I have important news. No, I'm sorry, no, nothing about the story. I gave it to Sheila Robbins and she promised to read it over the weekend. But that's not the important news. That's just what I told you I'd do."

"What's the news?"

"Oh," she said, "it's very big news. It's very wonderful news and I want to tell it to you before you tell me anything. Right away I want to tell you. And then, if you're interested, then we can do something about it. Unless you don't want to, in which case I'll hate you forever."

"What in the world are you talking about?"

"About me," she said happily, "and about you. About the whole magnificent world. Whee!"

"Is that the editorial whee?"

"You said it. Wheeeeee!"

He laughed and hugged her tighter. He kissed her again and her tongue flashed into his mouth, plunging deep, and he felt his passion beginning to burn.

"Pete, guess what."

"I give up. What?"

"I'm done."

"Done?" he said, stupidly.

"Done. Finished. Over and concluded. No more. All finished. Completely."

"That's good," he said thoughtfully.

"Now will you please tell me what you are going to do about that?"

He didn't tell her.

He showed her.

This time they did not go downstairs to her apartment. This time, since they were in his apartment, and since they were also in a hurry, they stayed right where they were. He walked to the light switch and flicked it off, plunging the room into something vaguely reminiscent of darkness. Then he reached for her, lifting her in his strong arms and carrying her to his bed. He threw her down on the bed and threw himself down beside her.

"Pete, it's been so damned long. I mean, enough is enough. Don't you agree?"

He agreed.

"I want you to do everything to me, Pete. Everything there is to do. I want to be kissed and touched and loved very hard. Do you understand?"

He understood.

"Ooooh. And I'm going to do things to you. Things that you'll like, Pete. I'm going to kiss you like ... *this* ... and touch you like ... *this* ... and do other things to you. Do you like the things I do to you? Do you?"

He did.

He opened her blouse and took off her bra, filling his hot hands with the cool sweet flesh of her big breasts. A wave of passion washed over her and she moaned softly.

His hands worked furiously on her breasts, manipulating the succulent flesh with the skill born of thorough familiarity with her magnificent body. She was warm and beautiful and she was his, his alone. Every bit of her beauty belonged completely to him, and he kissed and stroked her breasts with his heart overflowing with his overpowering love for her.

"Now my skirt. Take it off, Pete. Hurry. I don't care if you ruin the zipper, I don't care about anything. I just want it to happen soon because I love it so much. God, you have no idea how much I love it. And I need it, Pete. I need you!"

Then she was naked and he was kissing every bit of her. She groaned and squirmed with passion.

"That's good! Oh, Pete. Oh, that's so good. I love it when you do that to me. I love it, Pete. More! Oh, more because I love it so much. Keep doing it. Keep doing it, it's so good. I love it so much, so much!"

He tore his own clothes from his body and threw himself upon her, his body finding hers instinctively. Together and straining together, working together and moving together, reaching together and rising together and burning together and building together and—

"Pete! Great God!"

The sun went down and the moon turned black. The room was caught up in the tides of time, whirled by a force bigger than any other force in the world, the almighty and all-powerful dynamism of two people in love.

"Pete—don't stop!"

He had no intention of stopping. He never wanted to stop, never—he wanted to go on forever, a great gigantic and perpetual bout of love. He was in heaven and she was in heaven and the world had never been so good before.

"Pete, I love you!"

And he loved her, loved her completely and thoroughly. He loved the touch of her and the smell of her and the overwhelming goodness of her. He loved her, perhaps, because he liked himself when he was with her.

But whatever the reason, he loved her. And she belonged to him, and it was good.

Much later he showed her the story and told her how he had written it after deciding not to write anything that day. She read it and liked it, promising to take it in to Sheila Robbins when she went to work on Monday.

The night was calm and cool and clear. They had dinner out—plates of fish and chips at an English-style cubbyhole on Sullivan Street. They took the subway uptown to Times Square and wandered through the bookstores and shooting galleries and hot dog stands, looking at people and at things.

They went back to the Village on the bus, getting out at Tenth Street and walking the rest of the way.

"I like this place," she said. "These streets. It's a garden in the middle of the city."

"I've always liked it."

"But I don't think I could live here forever. I think it would get on my nerves after awhile. Do you know what I mean?"

He nodded.

They walked a little farther in silence. Then he said, "Some day we'll leave. Some day we'll both be tired of it here and we'll go somewhere else. Some place where we can have a house and a yard and trees."

She squeezed his hand, once, hard, and they walked on. They left the topic alone but now it was a spoken thing between them. They were not just a temporary alliance, not any more. They were a permanent thing.

They would marry and move out of Manhattan and raise a family.

That night they made love in her bed for hours. Their bodies took pleasure and gave pleasure and the world was good. They could not sleep, not for a long time. They would make love and it would be perfect and they would try to sleep. But when sleep did not come, he would roll her in his arms and it would begin again—the soft strokings, the warm wet kisses, the lips and tongues and hands doing the works of the gods.

Then once again the world would sing and dance and the sweat would pour from their steaming bodies. Again their bodies would shriek with joy that could not be held back. He was taking her, having her, possessing completely every bit of her body and soul.

She would close her eyes and love him, this man who belonged to her, who was her man to the end of time.

And he would whisper her name, the name that was dearer to him than life, and he would know with complete assurance how lucky he was, how much he had, how good it was for him and for her as well.

The night dissolved into day. The sun came up and rays of light snuck through the window into the second floor front apartment of 21 Gay Street.

And still they made love, still their bodies came together with frightening, devastating power.

Finally, with the sun up and day broken, they slept, warm with love.

CHAPTER 12

Monday was quite a day for Joyce Kendall.

At least a dozen times she reached for the phone on her desk, and each time she stopped just short of dialing the number. She wanted to place the call but didn't want to at the same time. She had to tell him in person.

And the minutes crawled by, just as they had done when she first got the job. Now, however, the minutes crawled for a different reason. It wasn't boredom with the job that made the hours pass so slowly. It was the excitement of life outside of her job.

Five o'clock came. Her desk was already cleared off and when the witching hour arrived, she swept up her purse and headed for the door.

"So long, Joyce."

"See you tomorrow."

"Be good, Joycie."

She hurried out of the office with the words of the other girls ringing in her ears. It was certainly different now. She belonged at her office, knew the girls who worked there, was friendly with almost everyone. Her absorption into the lifeblood of the office had been complete on Friday, when a new girl had reported to work for the first time. That made her other than the newest girl in the office, which made a difference. Before she had wondered how she could stand working at Armageddon for any length of time. Now she could not imagine leaving her job.

She didn't feel in the mood for the subway. She wanted to hurry home to Pete and tell him the good news. She looked around for a cab, remembering that they were almost impossible to find in the afternoon rush hour. But she had luck. A cab pulled up right in front of her to discharge a fare and she hopped in, giving the driver her address.

She paid and tipped the driver, then raced into the house and up two flights of stairs to Pete's apartment. She banged furiously on the door until he opened it—then she dashed inside and shut the door.

"Hey! What gives?"

"You did it."

His eyes went wide.

"This is to inform you," she intoned, "that your manuscript, entitled I WAS BLIND TO HIS LOVE has been accepted for publication in a future issue of *Desperate Love Stories*. I have put through a voucher to our accounting department for $150 as payment at our standard rate of three cents a word. You may expect a check within a week, Thanks very much for letting us see this script; we'll be looking forward to seeing more of your work in the very near future. All best wishes, sincerely, Me."

He stared.

"Sheila said it was just what the doctor ordered," she went on. "Said it was fine. I figured by then it was time to stop playing games so I told her your story didn't come in the mail but that I knew you and you had given it to me. That way I had a chance to hand her the new one. She's reading it tonight and I'll know tomorrow whether it sells or not."

He grabbed her and kissed her. He picked her up and held her high in the air, staring up at her lovingly.

"Hey! Put me down."

"You're sort of attractive. Did you know that?"

"Put me down, Pete."

"Why?"

"My nose bleeds at heights. Dammit, Pete!"

He put her down, laughing, and folded her in his arms. The kiss took a long time. Then he stepped back and grinned.

"I hope you own a fancy dress," he said.

"Why?"

"Do you?"

"Well, I have a frock that's fancy enough, I guess. But I don't understand—"

"Frock? That sounds dirty."

"—what you're talking about. And frock doesn't sound dirty. Sometimes you sound like an idiot."

"But you love me in spite of my faults."

"Of course I do."

"Besides," he went on, "I'm not acting like an idiot. I'm acting like an eccentric writer. There is, you see, a very tangible difference."

She sighed. "All right," she said. "So you're a swell-headed baboon. Will you please tell me why I should put on a fancy frock? And if you make a pun out of that one . . ."

He resisted the impulse.

"We're doing the town," he announced. "Dinner at Keen's. A

pair front and center for a good show. And more surprises after that. So get dressed."

"Pete," she said, "that's not necessary. You'll spend all the money before you get it."

"So what? We're celebrating."

"But—"

"Come on," he said. "Get dressed. Hurry."

"But—"

"Come *on*."

"Well," she said, "all right. I guess."

The steaks were rare, charcoal-broiled, and excellent. The play, *Of Crimson Joy*, was well-acted and very moving. The drinks at the Tavern on the Green were long, tall and cold, and they danced badly but happily to a Mickey Mouse orchestra.

Last of all came the hansom ride, which he had kept secret as a surprise for her. Sitting in the ancient cab behind the driver dressed in black coat and silk hat, listening to the clip-clop of the horse, they did the only thing possible under that specific set of circumstances.

They necked like schoolchildren.

The hansom dropped them back on Columbus Circle. They caught a cab for home, and on the way their mood changed slightly, shifting from exhilaration to a calmer form of ecstasy. Once again, though, they did the only thing possible.

They necked.

In her apartment, sharing final drinks on the couch, he cupped her chin in his hand and looked into her eyes.

"This is only the beginning," he said. "And it *is* a beginning. A small start but a start nonetheless."

She said nothing.

He took a breath. "I don't know how to say this, exactly. I guess I'll just plunge in anywhere. I'm awkward but, what the hell, I've always been awkward. Even as a child, when I used to fall off the sidewalk all the time. It's tough to fall off the sidewalk. But I managed it."

She kissed him.

He shook his head to clear it. It was funny—no matter how well you knew someone, no matter how deeply you loved someone, certain things were hard to say. According to the toothpaste ads, the hardest thing in the world was to tell a person that his breath smelled like rotten vegetables. That he could do with ease, but this was proving quite difficult.

"You liked tonight, didn't you?"

"Of course I did. Couldn't you tell?"

He reached for a cigarette, found a match and got it going. He drew smoke down into his lungs and blew rings of smoke that hung together for a long time in the stillness of the air. He wanted to speak but it was difficult.

"You like being with me, don't you?"

"Of course."

"And . . . would you like to be with me all the time?"

She opened her mouth but couldn't get any words out. So she nodded mutely, her eyes choked with tears that were ready to flow any minute.

"It won't be much," he said. "Being my wife, I mean. I'll never make a hell of a lot of money and I'm pretty tough to live with and I get vile moods and I snap at people and—"

"And I love you," she said.

"And you'll marry me?"

"Of course."

"That way we can move to one apartment," he said. "Somewhere away from here. And you'll be my wife and if I knock you up, we won't have to worry about anything and—"

"Shut up," she said, "and kiss me."

He obeyed quite willingly.

The wedding was small and simple. A Justice of the Peace performed the ceremony and two derelicts from Third Avenue specially recruited for the occasion served as witnesses. Pete slipped each of them ten dollars and let them wander off to drink his health until they were both happily stoned.

They honeymooned on Cape Cod. Joyce called her parents in Schwernersville, who cried, and Pete called an old army buddy, who happened to be drunk and hung up on him.

The wedding night was absolute perfection. It was not the perfection of a confession-story wedding night, with two virgins making each other miserable in a bed that was bigger than both of them. It was a union, complete and everlasting, of two persons who knew and loved each other with every atom of their beings. It was a full and complete union and it was very good.

After a few days of sun and sand they came back to New York. They broke their respective leases, forfeited their respective month's security, and moved their respective possessions to a three-and-a-half room apartment on West 74th Street near Central Park.

They both worked very hard, both at their jobs and at their marriage. Pete, as it turned out, was pretty much of a natural commercial writer. In a short time he was writing not only for the Armageddon confession magazines but for their men's mags as well. He would pick up magazines on the newsstands, read a few of them, and then slant a story their way.

"You need an agent," Joyce told him one morning. "Armageddon can't take half your stuff now. And keeping a batch of scripts in the mail all the time is ridiculous."

"So I need an agent. So who should I get?"

Joyce found out. She picked the best agent in the country and Pete sent over a pile of his stuff. Suddenly he had an agent. And things improved.

Joyce, meanwhile, kept working at Armageddon. She was a first reader for several months and then she was an assistant editor and before long she was an associate editor. She had an instinct for the business and she did her job well, enjoying it more every day.

One day she barged into his study while he was working, a habit he strove mightily to correct. "Hey," she said, "remember that book you were working on when we first met?"

"Oh," he said. "That one."

"I just read it."

"It's a dog," he said.

"The hell it is."

He leaned back in his chair, grinning. "I remember the book," he said. "It was going to be an earth-shaking powerful novel that would knock the critics on their ears. I'm pretty sure it was horrible. I haven't looked at it in a long time."

"An earth-shaking powerful novel it isn't."

"That's what I thought."

"A pretty good book," she said, "it might be."

"You're nuts."

She shook her head. "Really," she said, "I mean it. You started it as a straight novel, a hardcover property, and it's all wrong for that market, of course. The ideas aren't formed and the characters don't have enough depth."

"Other than that," he said, "it's good. That is, it's typed on good bond paper with a high rag content. Which ought to count for something."

"Will you let me finish?"

He grinned.

"Go ahead."

"I'd like you to give the book a reading," she said. "Think of it as a paperback instead of a hardcover. Same general background, a tighter plot, faster characterization, more punch. Make it an entertaining book instead of personal therapy."

"Ouch!"

"Well? Isn't that what it was?"

"I suppose so."

She sighed. "Write it straight this time. Tough and hard, with a good plot under it and some real movement to it. Then you can sell it. Isn't that better than keeping it in a trunk?"

"Much better. But—"

"What's the matter?"

"I never wrote a book before. Maybe I'm scared."

"Don't put anything on for me," she said. "I remember when you'd never written a confession."

"Well," she went on, "you remember what the Justice of the Peace who married us said? The old corn about all our troubles being little ones?"

"You mean—"

"I mean we have trouble coming," she said. "A little one."

He looked at her—his wife, the woman who was going to be the mother of his child. He reached out a hand and ran it over her stomach. He wondered how long it would be before the baby showed.

"You goon," he said.

"Are you unhappy?"

"You goon," he repeated. "How long have you known?"

"A few days. I wasn't sure whether or not you would approve. I—"

"Oh, Christ," he said. "Look, go put on a . . . a frock, will you? Now we have two things to celebrate. Move, woman!"

CHAPTER 13

The girl paid off the cab at the door and walked up the steps to 21 Gay Street. She was a short girl, just an inch or two over five feet, and she had very curly blonde hair. It was autumn. She wore charcoal gray slacks and a nubby yellow sweater. The sweater was tight on her well-formed breasts and the slacks were tight on her well-formed behind.

She made a careful search of her purse until she found the two keys that the rental agent had given her when she signed the lease. She tried the wrong key first on the front door. The other one fit and she opened the door and stepped inside.

She walked up the stairs, found apartment 2-A, and used her key—the other one—on the door to the apartment.

She walked inside, then closed the door behind her. Tomorrow, she thought, she would put her name on the mail box, stock up the refrigerator and do what she could to make the apartment a little more livable. It wasn't a bad apartment but it could certainly use a little color.

But that could wait. She was tired and she was all sweaty from her trip on the train. First she would take a shower and get some sleep. Everything else could wait until the next day, when she would be a little more in the mood for work.

She had no suitcase, only her purse. The rest of her belongings were in a trunk shipped by Railway Express. Tomorrow, she guessed, the trunk would come.

She peeled the sweater over her head, rolled off the slacks, removed bra and panties and socks and shoes. Then, slowly, she walked to the tub.

She was a very attractive girl.

The man in apartment 3-B, a recent arrival, was looking at pornographic pictures. He had a whole stack of them, ranging in size from 4 x 5's to 8 x 10's, and the stack included some very unusual material.

At the moment the man was studying the picture that showed two girls and a man. It was an extremely imaginative picture. The man observed the artwork, the composition and the lighting. Moreover, he observed the man and the two girls.

One of the girls was a willowy blonde. She was doing something incredibly clever to the man, while the man was doing something equally brilliant to the other girl, a stocky, busty, hippy brunette. If a person could judge by the expressions on the faces of the three performers, all of them were enjoying the whole affair tremendously. They were grinning like ghouls.

The man picked up another photograph. This one showed two women. The women were posed in the classic position of lesbian love, and a close examination disclosed that the models were the same two from the last picture. Again the man studied it very carefully.

Slowly, methodically, the man shuffled through the stack of

photographs, taking a long look at each. The more he looked, the more the pictures excited him. He decided that he needed a woman.

The man liked women. He liked to get them alone, away from everybody, and to make them do the things he wanted them to do. He had fun with women.

He wondered who his next woman might be. There was no way to tell.

For all he knew, it might be someone right there, someone in the same building with him.

Jean was nervous.

She had seen the girl, the girl who had finally come to take the place of Joyce Kendall. The girl was a curly-headed blonde with a delicious figure, and Jean was worried. She was worried because the attraction she felt for the girl was overpowering.

Terri was beside her, naked and asleep. She looked at Terri's breasts, at her hips, and desire came to her. Terri was sleeping but if Jean were to touch her, the girl would wake up. And then they could make love.

Jean looked at Terri and thought about the other girl, the one with the curly blonde hair and the delicious body. And she knew it was going to begin again, a sequence that could only end in some sort of heartbreak. She would make a pass—and if it was accepted, Terri would be hurt and if it was rejected, the girl with the curly blonde hair and the delicious body would hate her and run from her.

She closed her eyes.

She wished that she could sleep but she knew that she could not, not yet, not until something happened to relax her, to release her, to let sleep come to her. And so she opened her eyes again and reached out a moist hand, cupping Terri's full breasts, squeezing gently.

Terri woke up.

It was silent lovemaking, the union of bodies half-drugged with sleep. She kissed and stroked Terri's body and received similar caresses from Terri and things began to happen.

Half her mind rejoiced, singing with physical and emotional pleasure.

The other half wondered, curiously, what it would be like with the girl with curly blonde hair and a delicious body.

The girl woke up. She was used to cheerful surroundings, and her apartment seemed horribly drab now, drabber than it really was. Maybe she could paint the walls chartreuse or something, she thought. Anything to make the place more lively.

She got out of bed, got dressed. She opened her door and walked downstairs and out onto the street. Then she turned and looked back at the building, at 21 Gay Street.

Romantic. Greenwich Village, she thought. There was nothing so romantic about a broken-down old dump on a dusty street. The people who talked about romantic Greenwich Village had sawdust for brains.

She shook her head sadly. What a cruddy building it was! She wondered if anything exciting had ever happened there, if any-body the least bit interesting ever lived there.

Probably not, she thought. Probably not.

My Newsletter: I get out an email newsletter at unpredictable intervals, but rarely more often than every other week. I'll be happy to add you to the distribution list. A blank email to lawbloc@gmail.com with "newsletter" in the subject line will get you on the list, and a click of the "Unsubscribe" link will get you off it, should you ultimately decide you're happier without it.

Lawrence Block has been writing award-winning mystery and suspense fiction for half a century. You can read his thoughts about crime fiction and crime writers in *The Crime of Our Lives*, where this MWA Grand Master tells it straight. His most recent novels are *The Girl With the Deep Blue Eyes*; *The Burglar Who Counted the Spoons*, featuring Bernie Rhodenbarr; *Hit Me*, featuring Keller; and *A Drop of the Hard Stuff*, featuring Matthew Scudder, played by Liam Neeson in the film *A Walk Among the Tombstones*. Several of his other books have been filmed, although not terribly well. He's well known for his books for writers, including the classic *Telling Lies for Fun &f Profit*, and *The Liar's Bible*. In addition to prose works, he has written episodic television (*Tilt!*) and the Wong Kar-wai film, *My Blueberry Nights*. He is a modest and humble fellow, although you would never guess as much from this biographical note.

Email: lawbloc@gmail.com
Twitter: @LawrenceBlock
Blog: LB's Blog
Facebook: lawrence.block
Website: lawrenceblock.com

CPSIA information can be obtained
at www.ICGtesting.com
Printed in the USA
LVHW031150220322
714080LV00009B/803